THE FIFTH
BEAR HUG

THE FIFTH
BEAR HUG

James D. Navratil

Library of Congress Control Number:		2021901263
ISBN:	Hardcover	978-1-6641-5286-1
	Softcover	978-1-6641-5285-4
	eBook	978-1-6641-5284-7

Print information available on the last page.

Rev. date: 01/20/2021

To order additional copies of this book, contact:
Xlibris
844-714-8691
www.Xlibris.com
Orders@Xlibris.com
823621

Contents

Synopsis of *The Bear Hug* by Sylvia Tascher

The Fifth Bear Hug is a continuation of the stories in *The Bear Hug*, *The Final Bear Hug*, *The Third Bear Hug*, and *The Fourth Bear Hug*. The following is the summary of the first book.

The prologue of *The Bear Hug* begins at the new headquarters of the International Atomic Energy Agency (IAEA) in Vienna, Austria, where Margrit Czermak is copying for a Soviet security service (KGB) agent confidential documents belonging to her husband, Dr. John James Czermak, a world-renowned nuclear scientist and contributor to the development of the neutron bomb. Subsequently, the Russian agent sexually attacks Margrit, and as she is fleeing, her lover, Andrei Pushkin, intervenes and is shot by the agent.

In chapter 3, a red Mercedes-Benz roadster is seen inching its way around the Gurtel (Vienna's outer perimeter street), the driver eyeing the few scantily clad prostitutes who are soliciting their wares in despite the heavy snow that had blanketed the city. We then proceed with him to the third district, where a Ukrainian dance ensemble, sponsored by the United Nations' (UN) Russian Club of Art and Literature, had just finished its performance. During the cocktail party that followed, Andrei Pushkin, suspected by the U.S. Central Intelligence Agency (CIA) of being a covert Russian agent, captivated by a woman's melodious laugh, turned to gaze in her direction. He was immediately enraptured by the beautiful, charming Margrit Czermak gracing the arm of Boris Mikhailov, a prominent man with the IAEA, as he steered her in the direction of her husband. Meanwhile, two covert agents of the KGB, huddled in the background, are discussing the instructions received from the Kremlin to elicit from the prominent American scientist his knowledge of the neutron bomb, by whatever means necessary.

A few months later, on Margrit's return flight from London, where she had been attending her stricken brother, she encountered and was consoled by the compassionate Pushkin. In due course, he invited her to dine with him. As her husband's travel had again necessitated his prolonged absence from the city, in a state of extreme loneliness, she accepted Andrei's invitation.

In the interim, both the KGB and the CIA kept the American woman under surveillance, it being the KGB's intention to instigate an illicit relationship and the CIA's to use her to entrap Pushkin.

At the same time, John Czermak was suffering profound personal problems. While he had been employed in the nuclear weapons field in Colorado, his scientific endeavors had demanded first priority. As his present position with the IAEA had created substantial leisure time, he was both angered and dismayed to realize his wife's newly found independence. And being a man of high moral values, it never occurred to him that his wife was to become romantically involved with another man. To compound matters, he had belatedly sought to create an atmosphere of congeniality with his children, only to discover that he had little rapport with them.

With the passing of time, the clandestine liaison between the American and Russian flourished, eventually culminating in Paris and again in the Soviet capitol. However, realizing the futility of their relationship, they had on several occasions unsuccessfully attempted to terminate it. Meanwhile, the KGB, eager to record on film the boudoir events of the couple, applied pressure to Andrei by kidnapping his younger son. Thus, successful in obtaining the desired photographs, they were able to prevail upon Margrit for information relevant to her husband's work at the Colorado nuclear facility. During an assignation, a CIA agent met his death as he was propelled in front of a high-speed subway train. As Margrit had witnessed the event, an attempt was then made to eliminate her as well.

The relationship with her husband continued to deteriorate, and John made good his threats to leave her. Therefore, she beseeched Andrei to abandon his family to share a life with her. But Andrei had undergone a substantial ideological transformation during his affair with Margrit and, as a result, suffered continual agonizing self-debasement. Thus, he eventually took his own life.

Shocked beyond belief by the receipt of her lover's farewell letter, Margrit deliberated between life and death. Her friend, the Austrian Anna Winkler, who minutes before had heard of Andrei's suicide on the midmorning news broadcast, drove frantically to reach Margrit in time. And John, unaware of the morning's bizarre events but certain he wanted his beloved wife at any cost, rushed to make amends to her from the opposite side of the city.

Synopsis of *The Final Bear Hug* by James D. Navratil and Sylvia Tascher

The Final Bear Hug is a continuation of the story in *The Bear Hug*. The story begins with John James Czermak and his wife, Margrit, returning to their home in Arvada, Colorado, after spending almost three years in Vienna, Austria, where John worked for the IAEA. John is a world-renowned nuclear scientist and contributor to the development of the controversial neutron bomb. He returns to the job as manager of Plutonium Chemistry Research and Development at the Rocky Flats Plant, where parts for nuclear weapons are made. In Vienna, Margrit was romantically involved with Andrei Pushkin, thought by the CIA to be a KGB agent. Realizing the futility of their relationship, Andrei and Margrit had on several occasions unsuccessfully attempted to terminate it. But Andrei suffered continual agonizing self-debasement and eventually left Vienna for Canada after faking his suicide.

Following their return to Colorado, John and Margrit resumed a close, loving relationship that had been damaged in Vienna. About this time, John was recruited by Tim Smith of the CIA since John traveled to conferences around the world and to Vienna and Moscow to have meetings with his Russian coauthors on a series of books they were writing for the IAEA. Following more contacts with his Russian colleagues, John was informed that a background investigation had been conducted by the Department of Energy (DOE) and the Federal Bureau of Investigation (FBI). This investigation resulted in John losing his security clearance.

John was then granted a three-year leave of absence from Rocky Flats management to teach in Australia. Tim continued to keep in contact with John and asked him to visit certain countries and find out if they might be producing nuclear weapons. During his travels, there were several attempts on his life. After his return from his leave of absence in Australia, John started work in California. It was there that Andrei surprisingly contacted Margrit, trying to renew their love affair. Margrit rejected him since she had a good relationship with John and told Andrei she might go with him if she was a divorcée or a widow. This statement prompted Andrei to try and kill John, but instead, he accidentally killed Margrit. Back at his home in Canada, he learned of her death and committed suicide. In his dying breath, he told his son, Alex, that Czermak had shot him.

John wanted to start a new life and left California for a teaching job at Clemson University in South Carolina and even started using his middle name. Andrei's son, Alex, joined James's research group using a different last name. The story concluded during an expedition in Antarctica that the CIA supported to see if one of the Russian crew members was passing nuclear weapons information to a group of Argentinian scientists.

On the expedition, Alex tried to kill James but later found out that James did not kill his father. On the last night of the voyage, he met James at the stern of the ship and made amends to him, which ended by Alex giving James a big bear hug that caused both of them to accidentally fall into the rough and freezing ocean.

Synopsis of *The Third Bear Hug* by James D. Navratil

The Third Bear Hug is a continuation of the stories in *The Bear Hug* and *The Final Bear Hug*. The story begins in the later book with John James Czermak and his wife, Margrit, returning to their home in Arvada, Colorado, after spending almost three years in Vienna, Austria, where John worked for the IAEA. John is a world-renowned nuclear scientist and contributor to the development of the neutron bomb and returns to his job as manager of Plutonium Chemistry Research and Development at the Rocky Flats Plant, near Denver, Colorado, where parts for nuclear weapons are made. In Vienna, Margrit was romantically involved with Andrei Pushkin, thought by the CIA to be a KGB agent. Realizing the futility of their relationship, Andrei and Margrit had on several occasions unsuccessfully attempted to terminate it. But Andrei suffered continual agonizing self-debasement and eventually left Vienna for Canada after faking his suicide.

Following their return to Colorado, John and Margrit resumed a close, loving relationship that had been severely damaged in Vienna. About this time, John was recruited by Tim Smith of the CIA to see if some countries had a secret nuclear weapon program under way. It was easy for John to collect intelligence information for Tim since he traveled to conferences around the world and to Vienna and Moscow to have meetings with his Russian coauthors on a series of books they were writing for the IAEA. Following more contacts with his Russian colleagues, John was informed that a background investigation had been conducted by the DOE and the FBI. This investigation resulted in John losing his security clearance.

John was then granted a three-year leave of absence to teach in Australia. Tim kept in contact with John and requested him to visit certain countries and find out if they might be producing nuclear weapons. During his travels, there were several attempts on his life. After his return from his leave of absence, he started work in California. It was there that Andrei surprisingly contacted Margrit, trying to renew their love affair. Margrit rejected him since she had a good relationship with John and told Andrei she might go with him if she was a divorcée or widow. This statement prompted Andrei to try and kill John, but instead, he accidentally killed Margrit. Upon hearing the news of her death, Andrei committed suicide and told his son, Alex, in his dying breath that Czermak had shot him and wanted Alex to kill John.

Czermak wanted to start a new life and left California for a teaching job at Clemson University in South Carolina and even started using his middle name, James. Andrei's son, Alex, joined James's research group using a different last name. Ying from China also joined his group, and a loving relationship developed between her and John. The story in *The Final Bear Hug* concluded during an expedition in Antarctica that Tim supported to see if one of the Russian crew members was passing nuclear weapon's information to a group of Argentinian scientists.

On the expedition, James and Ying were married by the captain, and Alex tried to kill James but later found out that James did not kill his father. On the last night of the voyage, during a violent rainstorm, Alex met James at the stern of the ship and made amends to him, which ended by Alex giving James a big bear hug that caused both of them to accidentally fall into the rough and freezing ocean.

The story in *The Third Bear Hug* begins on the morning following the violent storm. A man and two ladies discovered James washed up on the shore of Cape Horn. They took him back by fishing boat to Deborah's home on another island. The couple was Deborah's neighbors, and she was a widow and retired medical doctor. She assisted James in recovering but found out he had amnesia and did not remember anything prior to being washed up on land. Deborah agreed to let James help her around her small farm. Several months later, the two started to travel to different parts of Chile together, and a loving relationship developed. James's memory slowly returned after an accidental meeting with a friend in Peru and returned to Clemson to have a reunion with Ying, family, and friends. The university appointed James as chairman of the Chemistry Department. During this time, Ying got killed in a hit-and-run accident that was meant for James. A week later, another attempt was made on James's life in his university laboratory, but he managed to escape the Molotov cocktail fire.

James was then contacted by CIA Agent Kim Carn, who requested him to go on certain trips to collect intelligence for the CIA. The last technical conference James attended was in Moscow, and he asked Deborah to accompany him. On the trip, they spent a few days in Vienna, where they got married. The Czermaks then went to Moscow so James could attend the conference. On the last night of the meeting, the two were confronted in their hotel room by a man with a gun, who identified himself as Nikolai Pushkin, Andrei's son and Alex's elder brother. Before he shot Deborah and then James, he said, "This is for killing my father and brother." Gravely wounded, James jumped over and gave Nikolai a bear hug, trying to wrestle the gun from him, but it went off putting a bullet into Nikolai's heart, killing him.

The story concluded with Deborah dying and James recovering. However, Andrei's brother, Alexei, was determined to kill James since he was convinced that James was responsible for the deaths of his brother and two nephews. The story concluded with Alexei attempting to kill Czermak.

Synopsis of *The Fourth Bear Hug* by James D. Navratil

The Fourth Bear Hug is a continuation of the stories in *The Bear Hug*, *The Final Bear Hug*, and *The Third Bear Hug*. The story in the latter book begins on the morning following a violent storm. A man and two ladies discovered John James Czermak washed up on the shore of Cape Horn, Chile. They took him back by fishing boat to Deborah's home on another island. The couple was Deborah's neighbors, and she was a widow and retired medical doctor. She assisted James in recovering but found out he had amnesia and did not remember anything prior to being washed up on land. Deborah agreed to let him help her around her small farm. Several months later, the two started to travel to different parts of Chile, and a loving relationship developed. James's memory slowly returned after an accidental meeting with a friend in Peru and returned to South Carolina to have a happy reunion with his wife, Ying, family, and friends. The Clemson University appointed James as chairman of the Chemistry Department. During this time, Ying got killed in a hit-and-run accident that was meant for James. A week later, another attempt was made on James's life in his university laboratory, but he managed to escape the Molotov cocktail fire.

James was invited to attend a technical conference in Moscow, and he asked Deborah to accompany him. On the trip, they spent a few days in Vienna, where they got married. The Czermaks then went to Moscow so James could attend the conference. On the last night of the meeting, the two were confronted in their hotel room by a man with a gun, who identified himself as Nikolai Pushkin, Andrei's son and Alex's elder brother. Before he shot Deborah and then James, he said, "This is for killing my father and brother." Gravely wounded, James jumped over and gave Nikolai a bear hug, trying to wrestle the gun from him, but it went off, putting a bullet into Nikolai's heart, killing him.

The story concluded with Deborah dying and James recovering. However, Andrei's brother, Alexei, was determined to kill James since he was convinced that James was responsible for the deaths of his brother and two nephews. However, Alexei was unsuccessful in killing Professor Czermak. John then returned to work at Clemson University.

The story in *The Fourth Bear Hug* begins after Czermak retired from Clemson, sold his two homes, and moved to Colorado. He then started working as a part-time professor at the University of Colorado and shared an office with a visiting professor from Moscow. He and Professor Lara Medvedev started traveling together to meetings, and a loving relationship developed. The last conference they attended was in Sweden. Following the meeting, they went to Moscow so John could meet Lara's parents. During this time, Czermak visited a good friend at the Russian Academy of Sciences, where they went to the roof of a tall academy building to take some pictures. Then Alexei showed up and tried to push Czermak off the building, but instead, Alexei fell to his death. Since John now thought that no one was trying to murder him, he asked Lara to marry him. She happily agreed. A few days later, they had a wedding reception at the home of Lara's parents. After the party ended and everyone left, Lara's ex-husband arrived to kill John but accidentally killed Lara instead. The next day, Ivan committed suicide after he heard of Lara's death.

Prologue

The U.S. Central Intelligence Agency (CIA) was founded in 1947. Its headquarters are in Langley, Virginia, and its agents collect, analyze, and evaluate security information from around the world for the president and cabinet. The agency also carries out and oversees covert action at the request of the president. The main priority of the CIA is counterterrorism, followed by nuclear weapon proliferation, and counter and cyber intelligence. CIA stations are generally part of U.S. embassies overseas, and agents are managed by a station chief. Some missions by the agency have dealt with regime changes in foreign governments not friendly to the United States, participation in the assassinations of foreign government leaders, arming insurgent groups, and illegal domestic spying on U.S. citizens. The CIA also uses U.S. citizens who travel widely to assist in collecting information pertinent to their mission.

One such citizen is Dr. John James Czermak, a nuclear scientist who assisted in the development of the neutron bomb when he worked at the Rocky Flats Plant near Denver, Colorado. The plant made parts for nuclear weapons. Besides being a nuclear researcher, he was a U.S. Army Chemical Corps officer teaching biological, chemical, and nuclear warfare to officer cadets. Czermak also taught at universities in Australia, the Czech Republic, South Carolina, and Colorado. He traveled to conferences around the world as well as first-time visits to many countries, some not friendly to the United States. He had many friends around the world, including Afghan, Brazilian, Iranian, Iraqi, North Korean, and Russian scientists. In both Colorado and South Carolina, CIA agents debriefed Czermak following most of his travels about things he observed that could assist the agency in its mission. Several times on Czermak's travels, there were attempts on his life while he was collecting information on nuclear proliferation and chemical and biological warfare.

Following his early retirement from teaching at Clemson University in South Carolina, Czermak returned to Colorado to start a new life after the death of his third wife. The murderer had intended for John to be killed. At Clemson, Czermak had been assisting Kim Carn, a CIA agent, in collecting nuclear proliferation information during his travels.

After John moved to Colorado, he started working part time at the University of Colorado. He shared an office with a visiting professor from Russia, Lara Medvedev. After several months of working together, a loving relationship developed. They traveled to Moscow so John could meet Lara's parents. They got married, and on their wedding night, Lara's jealous ex-husband killed her by mistake as the bullet was meant for John. Czermak then returned to Denver to try and continue living with the guilt that he was responsible for the murdering of his four wives.

Meanwhile, Kim Carn was transferred to the Denver office from Atlanta, Georgia. Her first assignment was to get information on a terrorist group arriving in several U.S. cities to disrupt American lives with simultaneous actions of putting poisonous substances in water supplies and in public places to shut down hospitals and transportation systems. Carn requested Czermak to assist in her duties.

Carn possessed damaging information concerning the White House trying to interfere with the next presidential election that her late husband had sent her before his assassination by a CIA contractor. Her husband was the CIA bureau chief at the U.S. Embassy in Ukraine and had obtained the information from an assistant to the Ukrainian president. The CIA director also had orders from the White House to employ the assassin to murder Kim on the grounds that she was a double agent, just like her husband, both working for the Russian government. There were two failed attempts on her life, one in Kiev and the other in Atlanta. Because of these attempts, she arranged to be transferred to the Denver office.

One late night, with no one about, Kim and James are returning to his apartment in downtown Denver. As they are walking, an electric car comes quietly and slowly pass them. John sees that the driver looks like Felex, the man who tried to kill him in the past. Several minutes later, they are startled to discover a speeding car with its lights out coming up behind Kim on the sidewalk. John pushes Kim out of harm's way, but he is thrown onto the car's hood. He sees that the man is indeed Felex, who is under CIA contract to kill Carn.

Chapter 1
A New Life in Colorado

I

On John's flight to Colorado from Moscow via Frankfurt, he catches up on writing in his diary.

Monday, June 1. I am sitting in business class on a Lufthansa flight from Frankfurt to Denver. The Boeing 777 is almost full of passengers, whereas the flight from Moscow to Frankfurt was only about half full. That flight took three and a half hours, whereas this flight will be about eight hours. My fare was doubled when I changed my seat from tourist class to business class, but I needed the privacy since I am still weeping every once in a while about losing Lara. We had been married for only a few hours when her jealous ex-husband attempted to kill me, but Lara had quickly moved between me and him, and she got shot and killed instead of me. There was a lovely memorial for her, where I also cried a lot. We both thought it was the perfect union of two people who had so much in common and loved each other so much. Besides losing her, I felt so guilty that she died saving my life. I should have died in my car going down Black Canyon in California instead of Margrit. I should have been in my car instead of Ying when Andrei's elder brother killed her by mistake. The bullet that Deborah took instead of me still haunts me. Now my fourth wife is dead because of me. I will never marry again.

The only good thing about this tragic event was finding out, the day after Lara was murdered, that her ex-husband had committed suicide. I feel so sorry for Lara's parents.

*They loved her so much, and it showed at the memorial. I am
sure that they will never want to see me again. Her brother
probably feels the same way. Oh, the guilt is so strong, and I
keep thinking of the mistaken deaths of all four of my wives.
Please help me, dear Lord, to lessen my grief.*

The flight seemed longer than eight hours since John kept
thinking about losing Lara. After landing in Denver the next
morning, John's renters at Pine Shadows, Randy and Gail, are at
the airport to meet him. They give John their deepest condolences.
During the hour's drive to Pine Shadows, Gail brings John up to
date on what has happened in Nederland during his absence. The
only important event was the nice weather and now the threat
of forest fires. John tells the couple about his trip and cries at the
end of his narration about Lara's death.

Right before their arrival at Pine Shadows, John asks them if
they would like to buy the property. He tells them he cannot live
in his home with all the wonderful memories of Lara. He plans to
retire from his part-time job at the University of Colorado, move
to Denver, and try to start a new life in full retirement.

II

The morning after John's return home, Randy comes to his
apartment above the garage and tells John that he and Gail have
agreed to buy Pine Shadows. John thanks him and starts looking
into property in downtown Denver.

After spending the day looking for a place to live in LoDo
(Denver's lower downtown area), he goes to Amy and Dave's
home for dinner in Aurora. Eric, Sylvia, and Lorrie also are
at dinner. The five greet their father and father-in-law with
individual hugs, and they each tell him how sorry they are about
Lara's passing. Over the meal, they all get caught up on their
activities since their last get-together.

John tells the group that he has sold Pine Shadows to Gail and Randy and has put a deposit on an apartment in LoDo. "It is on the top floor of a luxurious new building rising thirty stories above the site where Denver was founded. It is adjacent to the convergence of Cherry Creek and the South Platte River and is an easy walk to the Aquarium, Union Train Station, Coors baseball field, Pepsi Entertainment Center, Elitch Gardens Amusement Park, and the college campus. As you know, near Union Station, I can catch the free Sixteenth Street pedestrian mall bus to the capitol, art museum, and main library. The light rail for the airport starts at Union Station as does several other light rail lines to the suburbs of Denver, and of course, I can take an Amtrak train to anywhere in the U.S. Everything indoors is equally exceptional. It has underground parking for owners and renters, valet parking for guests, a welcoming lobby with attendant, a large workout room, sauna, hot tub, swimming pool, large conference/party room, and lounge with two pool tables. My two-bedroom apartment, that I will call Three Thousand, or maybe TT, since the apartment number is 3000, is spacious with bathrooms in each of the two bedrooms, and living, dining, and laundry rooms and kitchen as well as a large balcony with stellar views of the front range of the Rocky Mountains.

"I have a *Wikipedia* article about LoDo that I copied. Let me read the short article to you.

> "*LoDo (Lower Downtown) is an unofficial neighborhood in Denver, Colorado, and is one of the oldest places of settlement in the city. It is a mixed-use historic district, known for its nightlife, and serves as an example of success in urban reinvestment and revitalization. The current population is approximately 21,124. Prior to European exploration of the area, Native Americans, particularly the Arapaho tribe, established encampments along the South Platte River near or in what is now LoDo. In 1858, after the discovery of gold in the river, General William Larimer*

founded Denver by putting down cottonwood logs in the center of a square mile plot that would eventually be the current LoDo neighborhood, making LoDo both the original city of Denver, as well as its oldest neighborhood. Then, like now, LoDo was a bustling and sometimes wild area known for its saloons and brothels. During the horrific Sand Creek Massacre, it was LoDo where the heads of the slaughtered Arapaho warriors were paraded in victory. As Denver grew, city leaders realized a railroad was needed to keep Denver a strong city, especially when the transcontinental railroad bypassed Denver for Cheyenne, Wyoming. In 1870, residents passed bonds that brought a 106-mile rail spur from Cheyenne. Union Station became the place most people traveled into the city and LoDo would be the first part of the city they would see. This section eventually became Denver's Chinatown in the 1870s to the 1890s, only to be torn down during race riots. By the mid-twentieth century, what was once a thriving business area had become skid row. As highways and air travel diminished the dominance of passenger railroad transportation, the importance of Union Station, LoDo's most prominent building, waned. In 1988, LoDo became the Downtown Historic District that was created to encourage historic preservation and to promote economic and social vitality. During this time, the neighborhood began its renaissance and new businesses opened. Gradually LoDo became a destination neighborhood. By the time Coors Baseball Field opened on the edge of the LoDo Historic District in 1995, the area had revitalized itself, becoming a new, hip neighborhood filled with clubs, restaurants, art galleries, boutiques, bars, and other businesses. Pepsi Center, located on the other edge of the neighborhood, opened in 1999 and further established the neighborhood as a sport fan's paradise. New residential development came to LoDo, transforming old warehouses into pricey new lofts.

"My grandfather Czermak told me that when he and Grandma first came to Denver via Hamburg, New York, and Sterling, he worked in a wild saloon on Larimar Street. There were many fistfights there, and he always had to break up the brawls. Say, Amy and Dave, since you both work uptown, we need to start having lunch together occasionally."

"Dad, that would be great. How about on the Wednesdays of the first and third weeks of each month? Dave and I can meet you at the Brown Palace Hotel at noon."

"Okay. After I move into TT, I would like to have a housewarming party. It will begin at four a week from Saturday, and I hope you all can attend. Since I have two cars, Red, my jeep, and Whit, my Smart car, and I only need one, how would you like Whit as a gift, Lorrie?"

"That would be wonderful. I like the white Smart car very much, especially the excellent gas mileage. As you all know, it will be my first car, and I promise, Dad, that I will continue to call the car Whit."

"I had the car appraised at $3,000, so it is only fair that I give Amy and Eric each $3,000 as gifts."

All three young adults shout, "Dad, you are wonderful and the best father anyone could have!"

On the first Saturday following John's return to Colorado, Bob Stevens, chairman of the University of Colorado's Chemistry Department, and his wife, host a memorial party at their home in North Boulder for Lara. John's children and brother, a few faculty members, Gail and Randy, and a couple of John's friends attend the party. Following the memorial, John returns to his home in Nederland to start packing his personal things for the movers, who will arrive the next morning. The day before, he had closed on buying TT.

Two days later, John goes to his office at CU to pack his books and papers. During this time, he receives a call from Kim Carn in Atlanta, Georgia. She gives her deepest condolences to John in a weeping voice. John thanks her for her call. Before the call is ended, she asks him if he would like to continue assisting the CIA. "John, let me warn you again that some of these assignments can be dangerous. If you agree, I will send you information on your first assignment by overnight mail since this phone and emails are not secure. I will need your new address and cell phone number."

Of course, John agrees to help her.

The following Saturday night, John hosts a housewarming potluck party at TT that his family and friends attend. Randy and Gail are present as well as a few of John's former West High School classmates, some colleagues whom he worked with at Rocky Flats, and a few faculty members, including the Stevens. All of John's family are there, including his elder brother, Bill, and his wife, Kay. Amy and Dave donated a vegetable dish, Kay made a wonderful potato salad, Lorrie purchased rolls and a vegetable salad, Eric and Sylvia brought the dessert, and John was barbecuing hamburgers, hot dogs, and steaks on a grill on the balcony. From the thirtieth-floor deck, everyone enjoyed the wonderful view of the Rocky Mountains.

During the buffet dinner, the conversations were mainly about everyone's activities. John was the last one to talk, and he told the group some of his plans for retirement. "I have almost completed my flying lessons and hope to take my first solo flight in a single-engine plane out of the Longmont airport in a couple of weeks. I also want to prepare a second edition of my actinide separations book, work out at the gym, and explore Denver more. I also plan to make some trips around Colorado and attend conferences in the U.S. and overseas, mainly to see longtime friends. My next overseas trip is to Egypt next month to see an old friend."

After the meal, discussions, and several tours of the apartment, the visitors slowly leave after giving John their thanks for a wonderful party. The young folks clean up the kitchen, and after more conversations, they leave for home.

III

John's daily routine usually consists of doing his stretches, weightlifting, and swimming at the building's gym; working at the computer revising his book; continuing to learn Russian and Spanish; keeping up with his German and French language skills; taking walks in various areas of Downtown Denver; and every once in a while taking one-day drives around Colorado. When possible, he would have a meal with friends and relatives as well as his neighbors.

A few times on his walks, he would visit his boyhood neighborhood, near Speer Boulevard and Pearl Street, about a mile from LoDo. During some of these times, he would recall his activities before he started attending kindergarten. He had a tricycle that he would pedal around the neighborhood. One time he tried to ride his bike off a two-foot wall to see if he could fly, but the dangerous event caused him to cut open his forehead. The scar is still visible today. He would also go with friends down to Cherry Creek to wade in the water and go to a nearby golf course to look for golf balls.

John also made some visits to the library, city park, zoo, and art and historical museums. He sometimes attended a few ball games. Of course, after his solo plane ride, he took flights over Denver and the suburbs at least once a month.

On one visit to see her father, Lorrie read about one of his trips to Hawaii in his diary since she plans to go there with a friend following graduation. John had promised to pay for the trip as a graduation gift.

The flight landed in Honolulu on Sunday morning, July 1, at six with a beautiful sunrise in the distance. I was picked up by a SpeediShuttle and taken to the Ala Moana by Mantra hotel on Atkinson Drive. The thirty-six-story hotel is first class and looks like a Las Vegas hotel. I was lucky as I got to check in early. (It is usually 3:00 p.m.) After getting settled in the room, I took a two-hour nap since I did not get any sleep on the plane. Following my short nap, I went for a walk in the large indoor mall next to the hotel called Ala Moana. It has three levels, a huge parking garage, and the usual shops such as Target, Macy's, Nordstrom, Bloomingdale's, and Neiman Marcus as well as lots of restaurants. I had a big lunch at Panda Express in the food court. I then returned to the hotel for another two-hour nap, followed by washing and drying my dirty clothes in one of two laundries in the hotel. I was surprised to discover that the hotel has a Starbucks that serves wine and beer.

Later in the afternoon, I took a half-day tour of Oahu's east shore and windward side. There were six other visitors in the small tour bus: a couple from New Zealand, a lady and her son from Atlanta (the lady is a high school counselor), and two young Japanese men. On the tour, the counselor dominated the conversation with the driver/tour guide in a very loud voice. At various stops, the kid seemed to do things the signs told people not to do like "Please do not go into this area." I found out from the driver/tour guide that James in Hawaiian is Kimo. He also defined lots of common Hawaiian words. At one of the stops, he played the banjo and sang. The stops were Kahala and Diamond Head slopes and the "Beverly Hills" of Hawaii, where beautiful mansions adorn Kahala's beaches and the slopes of Diamond Head; Koko Head, the tallest volcanic landmark on the east shore that rises 1,208 feet; Hanauma Bay Lookout with a view of the most photographed places in Hawaii and where Elvis was filmed in Blue Hawaii; *Halona Blowhole and Cove, where the ocean geysers erupt and where* From Here to Eternity *and* Pirates of the Caribbean IV *were filmed; Oahu's eastern shoreline; Waimanalo beaches, recently voted the number 1 beach in Hawaii with its picturesque cinder cone islands beyond; and Nu'uanu Pali Lookout with a beautiful panoramic view and site of the ancient Hawaiian Battle of Nu'uanu.*

In the evening, I took a walk down to the beach. After admiring the scenery and watching all the swimmers and surfers, I went back to the main street. Kawakawa Avenue paralleled the beautiful seaside. I turned around at the Royal Hawaiian Center and went to the nearby crowded Cheesecake Factory for dinner. Following the wonderful meal, I returned to the hotel.

On Tuesday, July 3, at two in the morning, I boarded a Hawaiian Airlines plane for a flight to Pago Pago, American Samoa. The Sadie's by the Sea Hotel shuttle bus was waiting for me at the small Pago Pago airport and took me on an hour's drive to the hotel. There are three traffic roundabouts near the airport and no stoplights. The speed limit on the curvy road to the hotel in Pago Pago is twenty-five miles an hour most of the way. My room is good-sized and has a balcony overlooking the bay surrounded on three sides by beautiful mountains. I arranged a tour for the afternoon after a two-hour nap that morning.

My tour driver was Rory Wester, owner of North Shore Tours, and I was his only passenger. He also has another business, growing and selling a variety of trees and plants. He was quite interesting to talk with. He and his wife live on leased land on a hill. He grew up in Oklahoma. After receiving a bachelor's degree in horticulture at twenty-three, he came to Pago Pago, met a local lady, married her, and they had four children. Rory and the lady divorced, and he repeated that program several times, adding ten more children to his care. Now he has a fifth wife and no children by her. I guessed that he is in his early sixties. He was a very intelligent guy as he talked most of the time about various topics as well as all the following places we drove by or visited: Cape Taputapu offered the best illustration in American Samoa of wave action on older massive volcanic activity that created Tutuila Island; Rainmaker Mountain are two of five great masses of volcanic rock extruded as molten magma during major episodes of volcanism that created Tutuila Island; Matafao Peak is the highest mountain on the island; Fogama'a Crater is one of the very few illustrations of the most recent volcanism in American Samoa and contains clues to the sequence of volcanic eruptions in this portion of the South Pacific region; Le'ala Shoreline has an excellent exposure of a relatively young flow of basalt interbedded with layers of tuff, and the site also illustrates erosion by wave action and is covered with dense tropical vegetation; and Vai'ava Strait is a classic illustration of steep cliffs and erosion-resistant outliers formed by wave action on a volcanic landmass.

From the road between Au'asi and Amouli, we could see Aunu'u Island. There are about three hundred people living there, and they must get on and off the island by ferry. Rory said that the ferry had not been able to operate the past three days because of a storm with high winds and rain. During the tour, it had rained on and off.

At five in the morning on the Fourth of July, the hotel shuttle bus took me to the airport on Highway One for my eight thirty flight to Honolulu then Denver. The airport is on the southeast side of the island next to the ocean. My Hawaiian Airlines flight was full. I had the window seat, and a beautiful young lady named Britanica had the aisle seat next to me. She was nice to talk with. Britanica grew up on the island and got a bachelor's degree in microbiology in Honolulu. Now she works for a firm in Honolulu. She told me a lot of interesting things about Pago Pago, Honolulu, and her work. Her companionship made the flight very enjoyable.

Chapter 2
Some Activities in Colorado

I

John usually has meals with Eric and Sylvia every two weeks, either in Boulder or Denver. Most of the time, Lorrie joins them. She has started graduate school at CU Boulder. John also continues having lunch at the Brown Palace restaurant every other Wednesday with Amy and Dave. Over lunch, the main topics of conversation are about their activities the past two weeks. John usually has the most to say since he has lots of free time for various things. He would always relate to Amy and Dave about his day trips around Colorado.

"Last Thursday I got on HY-285 and drove to the road going to Pine, about halfway between Conifer and Bailey. Just before reaching Pine, I stopped at Pine Valley Ranch Park, a Jefferson County Open Space, where I took a three-mile walk on the narrow gauge trail where the train tracks used to run from Pine to Denver for a train transporting logs. It was a great walk with the wonderful sound of the North Fork of the South Platte River that parallels the trail. Following a drive around Pine, I drove on the dirt road that parallels the North Fork of the South Platte River to where it joins the South Platte River. There is an old abandoned two-story hotel located there called the South Platte Hotel. After some picture taking, I continued the drive back to Denver via Deckers, Woodland Park, Manitou Springs, Colorado Springs, and Castle Rock."

Dave commented, "My grandmother used to work at a saloon in Pine. That is indeed a lovely village with no more than two dozen homes. I will have to take you there sometime, Amy."

"On Friday I took a drive to Greeley to HY-34 to Wiggins, then took HY-144 through the small towns of Masters, Orchard, Goodrich, Weldona, and Log Lane Village. Before reaching Fort Morgan, I stopped at the abandoned town of Dearfield so I could have a look at the deserted buildings and take some pictures. After going through Fort Morgan and Brush, I headed south on HY-71, past Woodrow to Last Chance, a town of one home and a deserted motel and Dairy King, not a Dairy Queen. From there, I got on HY-40 to home. It was a great trip."

"Dad, it amazes me how you can recall all the details of your trips, especially remembering the highway numbers."

"You know I keep a diary, even of my day trips. Also, I have been on some of these roads before. For example, let me show you on this Colorado map the places I saw on a trip several years ago. I drove east on I-70 to Limon, where I got on a side road paralleling I-70. Then I drove through a series of small towns: Genoa, Arriba, Flagler, Seibert, Vona, Stratton, and Bethune. The next town was Burlington, which could be labeled as a small city. I continued east past the Colorado border into Kansas and turned around at the small town of Kanorado. I then went back to Burlington to have a walk around the old part of town. Next, I went north on HY-385 to the intersection of HY-36 then drove west. As you see on the map, the small towns I passed through were Idalia, Kirk, Jones, Cope, Anton, Lindon, and Last Chance. These small towns only had three to six blocks of deserted business buildings with several backstreets of homes, some deserted. In a few towns, there were no gas stations or grocery stores. However, every town had a post office. I thought the abandoned motels once thrived until I-70 was built. Most of the areas between the towns were farms with lots of corn and wheat fields. From Last Chance, I continued on HY-36 through Bennet and Watkins to home.

"Now I use the weekends for working at my computer revising my actinide separations book and doing chores around TT. I usually see Eric, Sylvia, and Lorrie about every two weeks and periodically have meals with some of my friends. I have also made some new acquaintances. Of course, early most mornings, I have a workout at the gym and swim twenty lapses in the pool, followed by breakfast.

"On Monday, I went on an all-day trip that started on I-25 to Colorado Springs. There was construction on I-25 between Castle Rock and Monument, and this stretch of the highway was stop and go. South of the Springs, I got onto HY-115 and drove past Fort Carson to Florence. From there, I took HY-67 through Silver Cliff to West Cliff. Then I had about a fifteen-minute ride northeast on a gravel road out of Silver Cliff to brother Bill's old home that he had built with no power tools. The cabin still looks great. Next, I took HY-69 through Cotopaxi to Salida, where I had a nice walk around the lovely old town with many beautiful historic buildings. From there, I caught HY-285 to Fairplay then went north on HY-9, over Hoosier Pass, to Breckenridge. Following a walk on the main street and dinner, I drove home on I-70. On the day's drive, I had seen herds of llamas, antelope, buffalo, and deer.

"Yesterday's trip was unusual as I drove to Georgetown in moderate traffic on I-70 and made a short stop at a point above Georgetown to take pictures. There I heard what I thought was a bear in the bushes growling at me. Then I hurriedly continued the ride between beautiful tree-covered mountains and past three lakes, over Guanella Pass, twelve miles from Georgetown, and Geneva Basin, two miles from the pass. There are still traces of two ski runs at the basin that now has a lot of trees on the trails. The ski area has been closed for many years, and all the buildings and ski lifts have been removed. This is where I learned how to ski in the midsixties. It was part of a required gym class at CU. The gym class in the fall was ballroom dancing. After arriving in Grant on HY-285, I headed back home, first through Conifer then on the road to Evergreen. A little later, I stopped to take some pictures of a couple of abandoned cabins and spotted several deer nearby. I got some good shots with my camera and then proceeded on a nonstop ride to Denver via Evergreen and Morrison.

"Tomorrow I plan to drive through Golden Gate State Park to HY-72, then at Rollinsville, I will turn off onto a gravel road that parallels South Boulder Creek and head west past Tolland to the East Portal of Moffat Tunnel. The only other route for train travel east and west is across Wyoming. A couple of miles east of the railroad tunnel is a narrow, rocky road to Rollins Pass. Thirty years ago, I could take the road over Rollins Pass into Winter Park. Back then, I had to drive through a tunnel and cross a narrow bridge that was very scary. Now only all-terrain vehicles and bikes can travel the narrow gravel road. After taking some pictures at the tunnel, I will drive to Eldora, a historic mining town. From there, I plan to drive home through Nederland, Boulder Canyon, and Boulder.

"I forgot to tell you at our last meeting about a trip I made a couple of weeks ago. Let me show you on the map. I went to Leadville via Copper Mountain Ski Area and over Fremont Pass and past Granite. I had a nice walk around the nice downtown area of Leadville and a short visit to the mining museum, then proceeded to Buena Vista. This time I only had a drive around the small town, then went via the Main Street to Cottonwood Lake that was fed by Cottonwood Creek. Uncle John used to take me, brother Bill, and cousin Don there to fish and camp out. After driving over Cottonwood Pass near Mount Princeton, I took a dirt sideroad to the small old ghost town of Tin Cup that had lots of old cabins with only a few people living there. There was a narrow gravel road that continued east out of Tin Cup over Tin Cup Pass to another ghost town, St. Elmo. However, the terrible washboard road had lots of sharp rocks, so I was afraid of a flat tire and turned around and headed back to Buena Vista. On the way back, I went by several deer and even saw a moose in a small pond. After I arrived back in Buena Vista, I went south through town and took a paved road west, through a resort area called Princeton. The road changed to gravel and continued several miles to St. Elmo. I had a short walk around the small ghost town of a few old stores and cabins. There was no one there, but a block or two away were a couple of occupied homes. I then returned to Buena Vista and took HY-285 back to Denver. It had been a great trip.

"I now have a goal of seeing all the cities, towns, and historical places in Colorado. My dad used to ask me why I wanted to visit other countries when there are so many beautiful things to see in Colorado. Before you both return to work, let me tell you some jokes I recently heard.

"In the Garden of Eden, Eve says to Adam, 'Do you love me?' Adam replies to Eve, 'Do I have a choice?'

"My ex-wife was deaf. She left me for a deaf friend. To be honest, I should have seen the signs.

"For Christmas, I gave my kid a BB gun. He gave me a sweater with a bull's-eye on the back.

"Posted in the elevator at work is the usual warning sign: 'In case of fire, do not use the elevator.' Scrawled in pen beneath it is this addendum: 'Use Water.'

"Anyone traveling on business for our company must fill out an expense report. A field on the form asks for the name on the credit card. One Einstein wrote, 'Master Card.'

"I was talking to my doctor about a weight-loss patch I had seen advertised. Supposedly you stick it on, and the pounds melt away. 'Does it work?' I asked my doctor. "Sure, if you put it over your mouth.'"

As Amy is smiling, she asks her father, "Did you hear how they caught the great produce bandit? He stopped to take a leek."

"A vegan said to me, 'People who sell meat are gross!' I replied, 'People who sell fruit and veg are grocer.'"

Both John and Dave laugh.

"Dad, it sounds like you are living life to its fullest by seeing some of the beautiful places in Colorado. Dave and I must return to work now. Love you."

II

John gets a phone call, and the caller says, "Hi, John, this is Kim Carn. How are you?"

"Well hello, Kim, it is great to hear from you. I have been fine, living in Denver in a great apartment. The next time we get together, I will tell you more about my new life in Colorado."

Kim asks John to photocopy the summary of his last trip to Egypt and send it to her by overnight mail. She said, "I assume you received my package a couple of days after my last phone call outlining the purpose of this assignment."

"Yes, and I am looking forward to seeing a few of my Egyptian friends."

"The Penny Group will be sending you funds to visit that country and find out if they are starting a nuclear weapons program, that is, if you agree."

"As I have done in the past, Kim, I will serve my country in any way possible."

"This trip could be risky, so please be careful. After the trip, you can stop in Atlanta on your way back to Denver and give me a report of your visit to Egypt. This pay phone wants more money, so I will sign off. I am looking forward to seeing you in Atlanta."

John makes a copy of his last Egypt trip write-up in his diary and mails it to Kim.

After arriving at the big Athens airport from Atlanta, I spent four hours in the airline lounge to have some free food and drink, watch TV, and check my email. The BBC TV news reported on some of the problems of the world. They also showed big piles of tumbleweeds that had collected around the yards of homes somewhere in Australia. The BBC newsman next showed a huge pile of the tumbleweeds in someone's backyard and commented that this was not Donald Trump's hair!

The Egypt Air flight took one and a half hours to get to Cairo. The plane passed over quite a few large and small islands on the way, and the first thing I saw was the Nile as we were approaching Cairo. At the airport baggage collection area, I was happily surprised to see a young man holding a sign with my name on it. He assisted me in getting a visa and took me to the Radisson Hotel in the hotel's van. The hotel is only about five minutes from the airport. At the hotel, my good friend Hesham was waiting for me in the hotel lobby. Hesham is retired from the Egyptian Atomic Energy Authority. I first met Hesham when he was a group leader. I was sent there twice for two weeks of consulting sponsored by the International Atomic Energy Agency, a branch of the United Nations. The work took place at the authority's research facility, about an hour's drive from Cairo, that housed two research reactors. Traffic in Cairo was even bad then, and sometimes the authority's shuttle bus would go up on sidewalks to pass traffic on the left. People on the sidewalks would scatter.

Hesham and I had about a thirty-minute conversation followed by his leaving for home. I then checked into the hotel, and after leaving my bag in the room, I went to dinner in the hotel restaurant. The next day was a holiday, and I just hung around the hotel until about three when Hesham came and took me on a drive followed by dinner. Hesham was driving a nice Toyota, and his driving was scary. During the time he had a high-ranking position at the Egyptian Atomic Energy Authority, he was chauffeured around and did not have to drive. During this trip, Hesham kept driving partly on the adjoining lane of traffic and going well under the speed limit. We were going to New Cairo that was designed from the ground up in a vacant area outside of Cairo. On the way, we passed a lot of apartment buildings, and there was rubbish everywhere. In one two-block area, there were many cars parked, and Hesham told me that the owners were selling them. New Cairo had many new apartment buildings going up and a large shopping mall that is like any in the U.S. Hesham and I ate at a place called Buffalo Burger and shared a Greek salad and a pasta dish. After a short walk around the shopping mall, we returned to the hotel. Although the Radisson Hotel is very plush, some things are still like a developing country: the fixtures in the room were falling apart, dirt everywhere, and slow service. I had trouble getting to sleep since my room faced a major street that was very noisy, mainly because of loud motorcycles speeding around.

The next morning, I had to wake up at six to pack and check out. Hanafi came to collect me in a taxi and took me to the Atomic Energy Authority's headquarters, about fifteen minutes from the hotel. There were four buses waiting there to take me along with about eighty other participants of the Eleventh International Conference on Nuclear Sciences and Applications to the Sonesta Pharaoh Beach Resort in Hurghada on the Red Sea. The buses left about thirty minutes late as was typical for the conference as everything seemed to start late. The bus ride took about six hours with a thirty-minute stop at a large gas station restaurant about halfway there. The ride was interesting with the highway going from six lanes to four lanes to two lanes. About two-thirds of the way there, the highway started paralleling the Red Sea on one side, and on the other side was flat desert and sometimes a large mountain range. There were two toll booths on the way. The bus also passed one large expensive-looking resort city. There were lots of apartment buildings going up there; I was told mainly time-shares. We also passed a few areas of oil pumping with refineries. At one place, there must have been a hundred windmills for electric generation. I was sitting in the front seat of the bus along with a middle-aged physicist from Bucharest, Dr. Cristana. We talked most of the way about everything, including her work and what I should see in the mountains of Romania. She plans on inviting me there in the future.

Hurghada is a city of about fifty thousand, and some of the hotels on the outskirts are very fancy. For example, one hotel called the Titanic actually looks like the ship Titanic. *The city reminded me of Las Vegas—there is even gambling here. There were a lot of buildings under construction, just like in the New Cairo area.*

The reception building of the conference hotel was pyramid-shaped, and there were wings of rooms going off on both sides. The balcony of my nice room overlooks a large swimming pool, and I could see the beautiful Red Sea in the distance. The hotel has several restaurants, a small shopping mall, and spa.

On the afternoon of my arrival, there was an opening ceremony of the conference. Later, everyone went to dinner. Since I was one of two invited participants (the other one from a United Nations agency in Vienna did not attend, and an Egyptian scientist had to give his lecture), all my meals and hotel expenses were paid for by the conference organizers.

The first morning, I gave my plenary lecture—"A Review of Molten Salt and Ferrite Processes for Treating Radioactive Solid and Liquid Wastes." My talk was well received with lots of questions after the talk. There was a two-hour lunch break between the morning and afternoon sessions, so I got caught up on writing about my adventures in this diary.

The next morning, I had to cochair a session on extraction and separation chemistry with an old Egyptian colleague, Professor Dr. Jacky. Other Egyptian scientists that I knew were Drs. Nerim, Soiry, and Noria. Dr. Noria had come to Clemson several years ago as my postdoc for a year. I also met several new colleagues.

The conference was chaotic, and even the session I was chairing started fifteen minutes late because of technical troubles with the computer and people coming in late. Then the first speaker went over the allotted time, and I had to announce at the end that there would be no time for questions. But then Hesham asked a long question, and the speaker took a lot of time to reply. This type of problem went on throughout the two-hour session. Even cell phones would go off periodically. However, after all this, the session was only fifteen minutes late despite another session starting fifteen minutes late that followed the first session. The problems and inconveniences were tolerable because the Egyptian people are so nice and accommodating.

The next day was the closing session of the conference. I got called to the front of the room, where I received a nice award that was a glass pyramid with an inscription of the society on it. In the afternoon, I joined Dr. Nerim and six others for a ride through the city to the dock area, where we boarded a small ship that had a lower galley with windows so everyone could look out at the sea and watch fish swim by. The water depth from the window was about ten feet, and we passed by many coral hills surrounded by beds of sand. The only fish everyone saw were small. One school of fish had black strips like a zebra. We were under water about an hour and then returned to shore so we could go back to the hotel by minivan.

On my last day in Hurghada, I took a walk around the hotel grounds down to the Red Sea and later walked down the main road to explore some shops at nearby resorts. Later that afternoon, I and several others went by minivan to the airport that was very new and nice. Security was extremely good as there were two checks. The flight to Cairo was an hour, and I had a nice view of the Red Sea out of the right side of the plane. Hesham and his wife were on the plane, along with several other conference attendees. Drs. Nerim and Soiry had taken the bus back to Cairo. Hesham's old driver from the Atomic Research Center was waiting for us in Hesham's car. We dropped him off at his home, and Hesham drove the rest of the way, which took almost an hour across Cairo loaded with rush hour traffic. Hesham dropped me off at the Holiday Inn that was close to his apartment. The hotel was first class, and my balcony overlooked the Nile that was just across the main street. There was a lot of air pollution, and I could not see the Pyramids as claimed by the bellboy.

After checking out of the hotel at noon the next day, Hesham came and took me to the airport for my flight to Athens, followed by a flight to Atlanta. It had been a great trip to a wonderful country with lovely people.

Chapter 3
Meetings with Kim Carn

After John's arrival in Atlanta from Cairo, he checked into a hotel near the airport. Following breakfast the next morning, he calls Kim and informs her of his arrival. She tells him that she will meet him in his hotel room in about an hour.

After their greetings, John tells Kim, "Wow, you have lost some weight and look great, more like Marylin Monroe than ever."

"You are as handsome as ever and still could pass for a tall Tom Cruise."

"As I have told you in the past, Kim, we should go to Hollywood."

"I was thinking on my way over here that I have known you since you first came to Clemson University several years ago. I value your friendship and all the trips you have taken on behalf of the CIA."

"I have also enjoyed working with you. However, I know you are busy, so let me give you a short summary of my trip to Cairo. I have also made a copy of my diary for your reading. I spent four nights in Cairo and was hosted by my good friend Hesham. As you know from reading about my last trip to Egypt, Hesham is retired from the Egyptian Atomic Energy Authority. I first met Hesham when he was a group leader. I was sent there twice for two weeks of consulting sponsored by the International Atomic Energy Agency. The work took place at the authority's research facility, about an hour's drive from Cairo, that housed two research reactors. Hesham took me there for a one-day visit on this trip, where I gave a lecture and had a detailed tour of the site. From what I saw and heard from Hesham, they have no intentions of building a nuclear weapon. Their research reactors are not equipped to make nuclear bomb material. Of course, Hesham and I spent a day at the Pyramids."

"Well, that is good news, John. I really thought since Israel is reported to have eighty nuclear weapons, although they have never confirmed or denied their possession of nukes, Egypt would want to have their own, especially since they were at war with each other in the past."

"Do you know what other countries have the bomb?"

"If you google what countries currently have nuclear weapons, you would surprisingly read that Russia has about 7,000, the U.S. 6,800, France 300, China 280, UK 215, Pakistan 140, India 130, and North Korea 15 to 20. Of course, one wonders where the authors of the report got their information. As you probably know, John, since 1970, 191 states, including the U.S., Russia, UK, France, and China, have joined the Treaty on the Non-Proliferation of Nuclear Weapons or NPT, an agreement to prevent the spread of nuclear weapons and promote disarmament. India, Israel, and Pakistan have never joined the NPT, and North Korea left in 2003. Iran started its nuclear program in the 1950s and has always insisted its program is for peaceful purposes."

"I recently read an article about Russia, the UK, and the U.S. reducing their inventory of nukes, while China, India, North Korea, and Pakistan are producing more. In 2017, the UN proposed a treaty to ban nukes, but countries with them did not sign up because the agreement did not take into account the realities of international security. The article also stated that while countries like the UK and U.S. are reducing their nuclear stockpile, they are still modernizing and upgrading their existing armory. It also takes a lot of money to continue to maintain the bombs since the plutonium decays in time and makes the weapon less effective. Rocky Flats was where the plutonium triggers were renewed. Now other DOE sites are doing the expensive job.

"Nuclear weapons release huge amounts of radiation, which can cause radiation sickness, so their actual impact lasts much longer than the blast. For example, the neutron bomb that I worked on was designed to mainly emit deadly radiation while causing minimal physical damage."

"John, I think Truman should have never ordered the nuclear bombing of Hiroshima and Nagasaki in 1945. There was huge devastation and enormous loss of life. In Hiroshima, eighty thousand innocent men, women, and children were killed, and seventy thousand were killed in Nagasaki, not to mention the long-term suffering of the survivors who were exposed to the radiation."

"Yes, I agree. Truman should have ordered the demonstration of the bomb in an isolated area of Japan where there would have been minimal loss of life."

"John, sorry to change the subject, but Washington has ordered the upgrading of the files of civilians assisting the CIA. So for the CIA's new records, would you please give me a summary of your entire life, starting from your childhood? Let me turn my tape recorder back on."

"I grew up with wonderful parents and two brothers and two sisters in a two-bedroom home in West Denver. I attended elementary and junior high schools near our home and West High at the edge of Downtown Denver. In high school, my grades dropped since I became more interested in cars and girls than education. I also worked at a supermarket part time. I dropped out of high school during my senior year to work more but went back the following year and graduated. I then started college studies at CU Denver part time in the evenings and began working full time at Rocky Flats as a janitor.

"As you know, the Rocky Flats Plant was between Boulder and Golden off Highway 93. Parts for nuclear weapons were made at the plant for many years, but now the plant is no longer there. It was decontaminated and demolished several years ago. Now the area is a national wildlife refuge.

"During the next three years at Rocky Flats, I was promoted to laboratory technician and continued part-time studies at CU Denver majoring in chemistry. To avoid the draft and being sent to Vietnam to fight, I joined the Army Reserve and took a six-month leave from Rocky Flats for active duty training. Half of the training was for me to eventually become a chemical, biological, and nuclear warfare training officer. A year later, I took a two-year leave of absence from Rocky Flats and attended classes full time during my junior and senior years on the Boulder campus. Following being awarded a bachelor of science degree in chemistry, I returned to Rocky Flats as a full-time chemist in the research and development department and continued going to CU Boulder full time for my masters, doctoral, and postdoctoral studies. After my university studies, I was asked to teach an evening chemistry course at CU's medical campus in Aurora, a Denver suburb. I did that for two years. During this time, I was promoted to manager of a group in the department and later director of the department.

"I am sure you have noticed that I have a handicap. I am a stutterer. I have had a lot of the embarrassing times as a stutterer, especially growing up. Some of my classmates used to make fun of me, imitating my stuttering. The worst time was when I was giving a graduate student seminar talk at CU. I stuttered through the whole talk. Margrit did not know I was a stutterer until a year after we were married. She had a calming effect on me. I have gone through several help sessions, and the flow technique works the best. When I get blocked on a word, I pause, take a breath, and slowly exhale as I say the word. Since my goal was to eventually become a professor, I joined a Toastmasters group and gave talks at high schools in the area. I also gave presentations at technical meetings and seminars whenever possible. Some well-known stutters are Charles Darwin, J. Edgar Hoover, Jimmy Stewart, Anthony Quinn, Elvis Presley, Winston Churchill, Nicole Kidman, Marilyn Monroe, and Joe Biden. There are four times as many males than females that have the handicap.

"I met Margrit Hoffman when I was in graduate school. We only had a three-month courtship before we were married. She was a beautiful, wonderful lady, and we were lucky to eventually have three great children—Amy, Eric, and Lorrie. I am sure you will get to meet my adult children sometime. Margrit was killed in an automobile accident when we lived in California.

"As you know, over two decades ago, I spent three years at the International Atomic Energy Agency in Vienna, Austria. In my previous work at Rocky Flats, I was a contributor to the development of the neutron bomb. In Vienna, KGB agents were trying to get information for the bomb from me via Margrit. She became romantically involved with Andrei Pushkin, thought by the CIA to be a KGB agent. Realizing the futility of their relationship, Margrit told me about Andrei and how they unsuccessfully attempted to terminate their affair. Later, Andrei committed suicide, and Margrit was beside herself with grief, but that event saved our marriage. Later, I was to find out that Andrei had faked his suicide and left Vienna for Canada to start a new life. After leaving the agency, Margrit, our three children, and I returned to our home in Arvada, a Denver suburb. Margrit and I resumed a close, loving relationship that had been severely damaged in Vienna. I also returned to Rocky Flats as manager of the Plutonium Chemistry Research and Development Group.

"About this time, I traveled a lot to conferences overseas and to Vienna and Moscow to have meetings with my two Russian coauthors on a series of books we were writing for the IAEA. Following more contacts with my Russian colleagues, I was informed that a background investigation had been conducted by the Department of Energy and the FBI. I was then subjected to several polygraph tests, but I failed all of them. I was puzzled by this, so I paid to have one performed by a private agency, but that test also showed that I was lying about a sexual encounter with a KGB agent. The FBI had received in the mail a picture of me and a lady I met aboard a Russian ship during a Russian Club of Art and Literature dinner. Margrit was a member of the club while we lived in Vienna. After the dinner, I was invited by this lady, whom I found out later was a KGB agent, for a tour of the ship. She took me to a room below deck and offered me a drink. Apparently, there was a drug in the drink that caused me to pass out. I had no knowledge of what happened next, but I am sure that was when the pictures were taken of the two of us without clothes on and in an embrace. I recovered about thirty minutes later. This investigation resulted in me losing my security clearance. I regret this whole episode in my life as it caused untold suffering to my family.

"I then went to Australia to teach for three years and later to work in California for three years. Andrei came to California and tried to renew his relationship with Margrit and kill me, but instead, he accidentally killed Margrit. I found out later that he committed suicide in Canada and told his son, Alex, in his dying breath that I had shot him.

"At that point, I wanted to start a new life and left California for a teaching job at Clemson University. As you know, I even started using my middle name, James. I enjoyed the academic life very much, supervising several students and teaching actinide chemistry. I even purchased the car and home that Margrit liked.

"Alex joined my research group using a different last name. I did not know that he was Andrei's youngest son. In early January, two years ago, I took him, another graduate student, and Ying, a postdoctoral student from China, with me on an expedition to Antarctica, where we would do some ice sampling. By that time, I had fallen in love with Ying. We were married by the ship's captain as we crossed the Antarctic Circle. The following night, me, Alex, and a dozen other brave souls camped out on Hovgaard Island, where there was an attempt on my life. On the last night of the trip, as we were crossing the Drake Passage and heading past Cape Horn, the sea was very rough, and large waves were coming over the front of the ship. Alex met me at the stern of the ship and with difficulty admitted that his real name was Alexander Pushkin, that his father was the one who had a love affair with Margrit in Vienna, and that his father had cut the break lines on my car in California with the intention of killing me and not Margrit. I was shocked as Alex admitted that on the camping night, he was the one who had kicked the rock that was holding me and my sleeping bag in place. As I was sliding down the hill, Alex told me that he was immediately sorry for what he had done and ran, trying to stop me, but that I had managed to stop myself at the edge of the hill above the sea. He also said that his father shot himself in his home in Canada where he was staying, and his father told him in his dying breath that I had shot him and that he should kill me. I sternly told Alex that I did not kill his father and have an alibi. Alex agreed and said he learned that morning that his father had committed suicide. Alex told me that he was extremely sorry that he had tried to kill me. At the end of our conversation, I informed Alex that under the circumstances, I forgive him. My last words were for him to come and give me a big bear hug. Alex happily jumped over and gave me a hardy embrace that caused both of us to accidentally fall over the back of the ship into the rough, freezing ocean."

John then tells Kim about Deborah, a widow and retired medical doctor living on Navarino Island, saving his life; his time in Chile; falling in love with Deborah; getting his memory back; and returning to South Carolina. "Upon my return to the U.S., Ying and I resumed our lives together, and I went back to teaching at Clemson. But later, Alex's elder brother arrived in Clemson and tried to kill me, but instead, he accidentally killed Ying in a similar manner as Margrit's death. A week later, he also attempted a second time to kill me but failed.

"In trying to get over my loss of Ying, I slowly renewed a loving relationship with Deborah, and we started traveling together. Several months later, while back in Clemson, I was invited to speak at an international conference in Moscow. I invited Deborah to join me, and we first went to Vienna where we were married. After our arrival in Moscow and my attending the conference all week, Deborah and I enjoyed the banquet on the last night of the conference. After returning to our room that night, Alex's brother surprised me and Deborah with a gun and shot both of us. Immediately after being wounded, I jumped over to the brother, putting him in a bear hug, trying to wrestle the gun from him. During the scuffle, the gun fired a third time, killing him.

"The police and ambulance came and took Deborah and I to the nearby hospital, where we were operated on to remove the bullets and then placed in intensive care. I survived, but Deborah did not.

"After Deborah's passing, I had another attempt on my life in the hospital that nearly succeeded, but I had a good nurse that did an excellent job of CPR on me. I knew it was Andrei's brother that tried to kill me, and I told that to the police.

"After returning to Clemson, I had several email exchanges with Misa, my best Russian friend. He wrote that the police continued their search for the brother but with no success thus far, and he would continue to keep me informed. I also arranged for a realtor to sell my two homes in South Carolina, and when I was ready, for movers to come and load my furniture and personal things for transport to Nederland. I then drove to Colorado so I could start a new life here.

"You know all the details about Lara and her death. Now I have started another new life in Denver and do not have any worries about any more attempts on my life. Kim, I know nothing about your personal life. Can you please tell me more about yourself?"

"First, let me turn off the tape recorder. I cannot tell you a lot because of my job. I grew up on Long Island, New York, and attended George Washington University for a bachelor's degree in criminal justice. Then I started working for the CIA after finishing my training at the CIA University in Chantilly, Virginia. My first post was in New York. After three years there, I was transferred overseas to our South African Embassy. I worked for Sidney Carn, the station chief. He was not an especially handsome man like you but had a certain charm and captivating personality that romantically attracted me to him. Our relationship grew, and we were wed about a year later. Of course, the agency did not approve of our union and transferred him to our Ukrainian Embassy. I remained in Johannesburg for a year before my transfer to Atlanta. Sidney and I have get-togethers every chance we get and, of course, spend our vacation times together.

"I am sure you can understand that I do not have any close friends because of my job, a lonely job, and only a couple of fellow workers have meals with me periodically. I have no relatives since I lost my parents and sister several years ago in a car accident. You are my only good friend. John, I need to return to work now. Thank you for your continued assistance to the CIA. I plan to be in Denver in a couple of weeks when I will brief you on your next assignment." Kim departs after giving John a hug.

II

A couple of weeks later, John receives a call from Kim telling him that she arrived in Denver the day before and would like to meet with him in the evening. He invites her to come to his apartment for dinner. Following their meal that evening, they enjoy the view of the sun setting over the Rockies. The main conversation was about John's next CIA assignment to Venezuela. "We have reports that the country is preparing to support a terrorist group in the U.S. Since you have some friends at the University of Caracas, we would like you to see if you can confirm these type of activities."

"One of my friends has some relatives in high places in their government. He may be especially helpful for any information on these type of activities."

"John, you know I spent some time in Africa, and I know you have made a lot of trips there. I have not seen much of West Africa. Could I borrow one of your travel diaries to read about your last trip there? I can return the book in the morning. And thank you for the wonderful dinner."

"You are always welcome to read any of my diaries. Here is the one you want. Let me see you to your rental car now."

That evening, Kim reads about John's last trip to West Africa.

I left Denver on the morning of Friday the thirteenth on a United Airlines flight at ten, arriving Dulles (Washington, D.C.) at three. After a three-hour wait, I left for Dakar. The South African Airline Airbus was full. I was sitting next to a young lady from Johannesburg who had been in Toronto for a wedding; she works for Toyota in Johannesburg. We were served a delicious pasta dinner. Later, I watched the old movie starring Michael Douglas, War of the Roses. *After not being able to sleep, I watched the very funny movie,* Ted. *The plane arrived in Dakar on Saturday morning at six. At immigration in Dakar, I had to get a visa. The immigration officer said the visa fee was $60, and I only had $45 in small bills, so I gave him a $100 bill. After he handed back my passport, I said, "Where is my change?" The officer then took me aside and asked me for all my small cash. I exchanged $45 for my $100 bill. Later, I found out that visas are free—another example of corruption in Senegal. I got a short hotel shuttle ride to the Onomo Dakar Airport Hotel. I checked in and, after a few hours' sleep, checked out at noon. After a nice lunch of the catch of the day, I went to the airport to board my Air Maroc flight to Casablanca at five.*

On the Dakar–Casablanca flight, there were three screaming kids in the next row. The kid behind me kept dropping the food tray and shaking my seat. After a half hour of the irritations, I moved to an empty seat at the rear of the aircraft. The plane arrived in Casablanca at eight, and I had a four-hour wait for my flight to Monrovia, Liberia. It was cold in Casablanca.

The Air Maroc planes, both old Boeings, coming into and out of Casablanca, needed maintenance and better cleaning on the inside. Luckily, there were no mechanical problems with the engines on the two flights.

The plane arrived in Monrovia in the dark at four in the morning. Fortunately, the hotel driver was at the small airport to greet me, holding a sign with my last name on it. There were only a few cars on the nice two-lane highway. I had a one-and-a-half-hour ride to the Mamba Hotel, where I had a brief stay. The hotel was good with a casino. I got a few hours' sleep before I returned to the airport for my three o'clock flight to Freetown, Sierra Leone. The return trip to the airport in the hotel car was much more interesting since I got to really see part of the city and outlying areas. I saw lots of unfinished cinder block buildings and homes as well as lots of shacks. Many people were walking along the road in the city as well as in several small towns that we went through. Most of the people were well dressed and were either coming from or going to church. Surprisingly, at the small Monrovia airport, there was a Delta Air Lines lounge in the Kenyan terminal (one gate), so I got some free drinks while I waited two hours for the one-hour flight to Freetown. On the flight, the plane flew over what looked like many rivers going to the Atlantic Ocean. Later, I would find out that most of the big lakes and rivers were just part of the ocean at high tide. The air over Monrovia was very smoggy, but it improved near Freetown.

At the Freetown airport, I exchanged $100 for seventy-three ten thousand Leone bills. I felt like a rich man trying to get the stack of bills into my pocket. I thought the hotel shuttle bus would be waiting for me at the airport, but after talking to several people, I found out that I had to buy a ferry ticket. Lungi International Airport is separated from Freetown City by a broad eighteen-mile river channel. I finally found the hotel host who took me to the sales desk of *the Sea Bird Boat Service at the airport terminal. I and ten others were transported by coach to the jetty five minutes away. After a long wait, we boarded a speedboat for a wild ride across the river channel to the shore on the western side of the city. The ride took about forty-five minutes over very choppy waters. There, I got a ride on a hotel shuttle bus to the hotel through lots of traffic. I was told that there is a highway connecting the airport with the city, but the ride takes more than three hours. I plan to take that method of transportation on my return to the airport so I can see more of the country.*

The Swiss Spirit Hotel Freetown is in a trendy residential area of the city, close to the beautiful and white sandy stretch of Lumley Beach, where the golf club is located. After my arrival at the hotel at six and check-in, I went to a nice room with two single beds, a desk, a couch, and a balcony overlooking the ocean. That evening, I had a nice dinner of fish and chips. I got acquainted with a couple at the next table who were from New York. They told me a little about Freetown and what I should be sure and see. There was also a group of about a dozen Americans in the restaurant that was attending some type of church activity and meeting at the hotel.

The next morning, I booked a three-hour tour of the city. My driver/guide, Larry, had grown up in Freetown and knew the city well. Larry spoke excellent English as did most of the people I met. He had a Toyota 4-wheeler, and we first went to the highest mountain that overlooked the city with fantastic views of the city and ocean; I took lots of pictures. Next, Larry drove into the city, where there were many shops and crowds of shoppers. We cruised by several beautiful churches and a couple of mosques. Most buildings looked good, but others were in bad shape with windows broken or gone. We then took a long drive out to a white sandy beach. There were lots of school kids going to or from school since they have two schedules; one group goes to school in the morning and the other half in the afternoon. They all wear the same type of uniforms. Larry says English is taught in school as well as their native tongue. Along the roadsides in many places are shacks with various vendors selling everything one would need, including African artwork and wooden masks and statues. In places, there were big fancy homes on the mountainsides, along with small tin sheds where people were living. We stopped at Larry's uncle's home on the way back to town, and his home is like a mansion. His uncle had worked in Switzerland several years and brought back his savings. Now his uncle manages a construction company. After a short visit with his uncle, Larry took me back to the hotel. I arranged for him to take me to the airport in the morning.

The next day, Larry collected me at the hotel. We first drove through town and passed the main mountain we had been to yesterday. Traffic was not bad. The skies were blue, and it was warm. The drive to the airport would take four hours. After we got out of Freetown and near a small village, the Toyota's check engine light came on. Larry stopped, shut off the engine, and opened the hood to check the engine. He shut the hood and tried to start the Toyota without success. He told me to sit tight while he went for help. Larry waved down a motorcyclist, and off the two of them went. I was worried and spent most of the half hour while Larry was away praying. During that time, I spoke with four young ladies who were selling water nearby. Larry came back in a car with a mechanic who had a battery and jumper cables. They got the Toyota started, and we followed the mechanic back to his shop, where they tried to find why the battery was dead. After fifteen to twenty minutes of trying to find the problem, they jump-started the Toyota, and we were back on the highway to the airport with both of us worrying that engine trouble might happen again.

On the trip, we went through several small villages and the second-largest city in Sierra Leone. At the city, the main road went to Liberia, but we continued on another highway toward Guinea. In general, the highways were in good shape except in a couple of places where they were building another lane, and we had to go over some very bumpy red dirt roads. Many school kids were walking along the highway near the villages. There were also many small shacks on the roadsides in the villages selling everything from firewood to water. The homes were a variety of large beautiful ones to small grass-covered mud brick homes. There were lots of goats grazing near the roadside, and they seemed to know to keep off the highway. Most of the villages had speed bumps on both ends of the village.

We got to the airport without any problems. Larry was a good driver. I wondered how Larry would get back to the hotel on the ferry when he would probably have to shut the engine off.

I regret leaving the hotel at ten that morning since my Air France flight to Conakry did not leave until nine in the evening. After waiting two hours to get checked in, I went upstairs to the airport lounge. The American couple I met yesterday was on my flight, but they will stay on the plane in Conakry that goes onto Paris. In Paris, they will catch their flight to New York. We had a long wait at the four-gate airport. The flight left on time, and I was in seat 4A, first class. The plane arrived in Conakry, Guinea, about forty-five minutes later. The Conakry airport has Jetways, so it was the first West African airport that I did not have to use the stairs to get off the plane and bused to the terminal.

The Sheraton Grand Conakry shuttle bus driver was waiting for me and another passenger in the arrivals hall. It turned out that the other passenger was the Frenchman who sat next to me on the flight. After check-in at the hotel, I went to the restaurant for dinner before going to my room.

The hotel is five star, has eleven floors and many rooms. It is a beautiful hotel and the first one so far that had a business center where I could check my email. The hotel also has a spa, a gym, and three restaurants. My balcony overlooks the pool and bar area that is next to the Atlantic Ocean. There are no rooms on the other side of the wide hallway. Instead, there are windows that provide a great easterly view of the large city with lots of new homes and buildings being built.

After breakfast the next morning, Wednesday, January 18, I arranged for a car and driver to take me to see the city for about two hours. Later, I watched Euro News and surprisingly heard that their president had declared a state of emergency. He had lost the recent election but would not leave office as he declared that the election was rigged. Euro News reported that thousands of people were fleeing to Senegal. When I went to the hotel last night, there were lots of people out enjoying themselves at roadside bars and restaurants, so this bad and scary news was surprising.

I was picked up by my driver, Sherf, at one. He drives a four-wheel drive Kia and is married and has a young daughter. We headed downtown so I could exchange some money at a bank, go to the post office, and then buy a baseball cap. It took almost an hour to get downtown because of traffic and to periodically slow down to get over potholes. We passed many roadside stalls selling everything, just like in Freetown and Monrovia. Most buildings were two to four stories, some in good shape and others not so good. We went through some poor areas of the city where it looked like people were living in shacks. I thought to myself that I could never drive here as traffic was chaotic like Cairo, Tripoli, Monrovia, and Freetown. Surprisingly, I saw no accidents. When we got to the post office in the middle of the downtown area, trying to find a parking space was a challenge for Sherf. He found a place about two blocks away from the post office, and typical of the whole city, there were *only sidewalks in some places. Sherf and I had to walk in the street and try to avoid getting hit by cars and motorcycles. Across from the post office were several guys exchanging money. Sherf said the banks would be too busy, so this was the best I could do for my transaction. I exchanged $20 for about 10,000 Guinean francs. After paying for ten postcards with stamps, I had only one 5,000 note left.*

A block in the other direction of the car was a sport shop. Luckily, they had a cap with Guinea on it; I had finally lucked out, unlike in Monrovia and Freetown, to add this hat to my collection. The clerk only wanted $5 for it. Sherf next drove more around the center of town, then back near the Sheraton, and continued past the airport and around a poor section of the city. Again, traffic was wild as we approached rush hour. I wondered how all the shop vendors, especially the ones selling the same things, made a living. There were also street vendors, mostly women with baskets of peanuts and chips on their heads, and others selling small plastic bags of drinking water. Most of the young men were selling boxes of Kleenex, CDs, and sunglasses. In certain parts of town were small roadside shops where furniture was made and displayed outside. The furniture was beautiful, and one bed headboard and footboard were made of carved marble. Other stores in one area were selling plastic baskets and pots.

I saw no Caucasians on the four-hour city tour, and there are only about a dozen Caucasians at the hotel, including four Chinese businessmen. We got back to the hotel at five. By the way, Sherf speaks fairly good English. He only wanted $50 for the tour, but I only had $100 notes, so I gave Sherf 50 euros. He plans to pick me up after lunch tomorrow for another tour. In the evening, I got caught up on this diary, wrote postcards, watched a beautiful sunset, and had dinner.

On Thursday, after breakfast and checking my email, I wrote more postcards and watched CNN. Today the news reports that it was the Gambian president who will not step down, not the president of Guinea. That is why I saw no unrest or protests during the city tour yesterday. The other news was about an earthquake that caused avalanches in Central Italy. After checking out of the hotel at one, Sherf picked me up for an additional drive around the city and outlying areas before taking me to the airport. On the drive, Sherf took me toward Coxa Mountain, north of the city. We went through several suburban areas. Again, there were many buildings under construction, roadside stalls selling everything from fruit and vegetables to shoes, appliances, and furniture. I saw lots of small children, some playing with balls or pushing tires around. Most people were well dressed and seemed happy. I saw lots of smiles and lots of stares at my tanned face.

At the Conakry airport, there was a small group of white businessmen and a group of what looked like young Tibetan men. There was a beautiful yellow-and-white cat walking around. I even saw a mouse in the airport lounge and gave him some of my sandwich. I spoke with a fellow passenger who works for the World Bank. He told me that they funded the building of the Sheraton Hotel since no other banks would.

I left Conakry at 7:45 p.m. and arrived in Dakar at 9:10 p.m. on a Brussels Airlines flight. After landing, the plane would continue on to Brussels. I had to go through immigration and customs as there was no transit exit. The wait was long at immigration, but this time the officer did not ask for a visa fee, probably since there were lots of people around. I had to wait until 2:30 a.m. for my flight, but it was not bad since the airline lounge was good. I could not sleep on the nine-hour flight to D.C. as the only two children on the plane, ages about two and four, cried and made loud noises during most of the flight. Furthermore, the two TVs did not work. I had both the window and aisle seats to myself.

On the flight, I was reflecting on this wonderful West African trip. I was amazed how they got Ebola under control with all the hundreds of people closely intermingling in the cities. Nigeria got their Ebola outbreak quickly under control before my visit there two years ago. The Sheraton Hotel was one of the best I have stayed in, but it did cost 500 euros for the two nights.

Kim decides to read about John's previous trip to West Africa and Europe.

After arriving in Lisbon from Denver via D.C., I overnighted at a hotel near the airport. The next morning, I took a TAP airline flight from Lisbon to São Tomé. São Tomé is the largest island of São Tomé and Principe. It is off the coast of the Atlantic Ocean in the Gulf of Guinea, west of Gabon, and straddles the Equator. The nation was discovered and claimed by Portugal in the fifteenth century, and the island's sugar-based economy gave way to coffee and cocoa in the nineteenth century. Slave labor was used that lingered into the twentieth century. Although independence was achieved in 1975, democratic reforms were not instituted until the late 1980s, and the first free elections were held in 1991. Portuguese is the main language, and 80 percent of the people are Catholic. About two-thirds of the young population are girls.

The flight to São Tomé took about seven hours with a stop in Accra to let out about two-thirds of the passengers. During the plane's descent into São Tomé about five, I saw that the island looked genuinely nice and green with some mountains and green bays. One other plane was at the small airport, and there is only one runway used for both takeoffs and landings. I got my visa at the airport. The

Pestana Hotel shuttle bus was waiting outside the arrivals hall and took me and several other passengers to the hotel. I got to see most of the small city as the hotel was on the other side of town.

The new five-star hotel is exceptionally large and modern, with two large swimming pools and garden, and it sits next to the ocean. There is a casino next door that is not too big. I got five dobra tokens as a gift from the hotel to play the slots. Of course, I lost all the coins at one time on one slot that night. As usual, I arranged a tour of the island for the next day. My tour guide was Waciley and my driver Amid. Both gentlemen spoke good English. Waciley's wife is a medical doctor, and they have two young girls. The tour took about four hours. Waciley told me that he had never been to Principe, the smaller island; he said it was less than an hour by plane and four hours by ferry. I asked how long does it take to swim there. With a smile on his face, Waciley said about two days. He also told me that crime was nonexistent.

We first went north along the ocean, passing many beautiful beaches, then northwest into the interior. The island is covered by a lush rainforest and is a veritable paradise with many banana, sugarcane, coffee, and cocoa trees and plants. Many former plantations are now covered with forest, and there are many abandoned sugar mills. The interior contains Obo National Park, where the extinct Pico de São Tomé volcano is located. We went to the secluded São Nicolau waterfall, saw many different kinds of birds and lots of orchids, and on the way back to town stopped at the Monte Café to see the coffee museum and greenhouses where coffee plants are grown.

Back in town, we went by many colorful colonial-style buildings and old Portuguese statues and through the busy market. We had a stop at Independence Square. We also visited Fort São Sebastião that was built in 1575; it had been refurbished in 2006 and is now a museum.

The next morning, I continued on the tour with Waciley and Amid. Amid drove south, paralleling the ocean. We first went to see the Boca do Inferno blowhole on the south side of the island. Farther south was a slim upside-down, cone-shaped mountain standing alone. Very unusual. We passed several rivers where the native ladies were washing their clothes. To dry the clothes, they just laid the garments on the grass. We passed through several villages, and there were lots of groups of school kids on their way home from school. There are two shifts of school times, one in the morning and the other one in the afternoon. Some of the kids waved to us as we went by. We also visited a large abandoned plantation house that was built in the 1600s, where Waciley said he was born. There was a group of young girls there that loved getting their picture taken. They asked me for candy and pens for school, but of course, I had nothing to give them. The kids were all dressed the same, in nice uniforms.

The roads were exceptionally good in most places, and I saw lots of dogs, cats, goats, pigs, and one cow but no monkeys. There are no horses on the island. We also had a tour of a working cocoa mill, and again, a couple of groups of children were asking for candy and school supplies. Next time I will bring some ballpoint pens with me. I would like to visit Principe on my next trip to Africa.

That evening, the hotel shuttle bus took me along with about a dozen other guests, mainly Portuguese tourists, to the small airport to catch our nine thirty flight to Lisbon. There was only one room in the departure hall that had a small gift shop and even smaller café. Security was good; the agents were even going through checked luggage. It looked like some passengers had all their worldly possessions with them.

On the layover in Acura, one of the passengers had a heart attack. Luckily, there were three doctors on board. After about a half hour, an ambulance came and took him off the aircraft. The plane arrived in Lisbon about seven the next morning, and two hours later, I caught my SATA Air flight to Terceira, Azores, the second-largest island after São Miguel that I had visited in February.

The Terceira airport is new and nice and about ten miles northwest from Angra do Heroísmo, the largest town, where I would be staying. The second-largest town, Praia Da Vitória, is on the east side of the island, much closer to the airport. The two towns and airport are all right next to the Atlantic Ocean. During the taxi ride, the car was on a nice double lane highway, and we passed many farms with volcanic rock walls separating the one to two-acre pastures, many with dairy cows eating the rich grass. There were many rolling green hills, just an absolutely beautiful island of fifty-six thousand people. Angra do Heroísmo has a population of about five thousand. The taxi driver told me that there is a U.S. Army airbase nearby with about two hundred American airmen stationed there. He said the number of men used to be a lot higher.

I stayed at the large and fairly new four-star Terceira Mar Hotel, next to the ocean. Across the bay is Monte Brasil that has an old fortress on it. The fortress is still used by the military. I got a nice room that looked over the sea to the right and to the left the hotel grounds, tennis court, and swimming pool, with the fortress and mountains beyond. In the afternoon, I took a fifteen-minute walk into the downtown. Most of the buildings are of stucco and painted in a variety of colors with red tile roofs. The streets had overhead decorations connected to the streetlights. There were a couple of beautiful churches and an adjoining bay with lots of sailing ships docked. Music was playing, and food booths were everywhere as they were having Sanjoaninas

Festival, which ran from June 17 to 26. Each day there was a different event taking place. I had just missed the bullfights, and yesterday was a water-skiing event.

The next morning, my beautiful driver and guide, Maria Kones, picked me up for a tour of the island. She has a university degree in tourism that she got in Lisbon, and her boyfriend takes care of cows. She said that tourism is the number 2 industry after farming. Our first stop was on top of Monte Brasil, where we had a wonderful view of the fortress, hotel, and town. There was a shooting range for the army nearby, where I spoke with an American who had been born on the island, moved with his folks to Boston when he was ten, and had just returned permanently after forty years of living in Boston. He said he loved Boston, but this island paradise more than Boston. Next, we went through town and up the coast through São Sebãstiao and Porto Martins to Praia da Vitória for a drive around the town and lunch. Maria and I ate lunch at an old restaurant full of ancient relicts and antiques. Then we went northwest across the middle of the island. At one point, we crossed a large hill with many cows behind rock walls and ended up behind a young man trying to move a small herd of cows down the one-lane road. After a while, he finally got the cows into a field so we could proceed on our way through several small villages. In this area are farms growing grapes, and the interesting thing was that each couple of rows of grapes is lined with volcanic rock walls to keep the grapes warm at night. Our final stop was a visit to the Algar do Carvão, an extinct volcano that sits about the middle of the island. It is the only one in the world where one can go through a cave and down about three hundred stairsteps to the caldera and look up and see the round hole of the volcano. It had been a very enjoyable tour, thanks to Maria.

On June 20, I returned to Lisbon and overnighted at the Nacional again. The next morning, I flew via London and

Aberdeen to Sumburgh, Shetland Islands, arriving about four. On the flight, I got acquainted with Mods Barren, executive vice president of Deep Ocean, an offshore oil and gas company based in Haugesund, Norway. He was going to Lerwick for a meeting and was staying at the same hotel, the Shetland, as I was. There was a driver and car waiting for him, and he gave me a ride to the hotel, along with a couple of his coworkers who were also planning on attending the meeting. The driver dropped the coworkers off at another hotel before going to the Shetland.

The next morning, I took a walk into the downtown area of Lerwick. I was glad I was wearing my light jacket since it was quite cool, even though the sun was out. Lerwick has a population of about eight thousand, where the island supports twenty million people. The main occupation of the inhabitants of the island is oil and gas recovery from the ocean. I spoke with several locals about the referendum that was taking place in two days to decide if the UK should leave the EU. Although I had some trouble understanding these locals, I found out that they favored staying in the EU and leaving the UK to form their own country again. An American lady, who also holds UK citizenship, told me that crime is nonexistent on the island and that they did not like Trump because of all the cheating he did in building a golf course in Scotland. (Trump arrived a few days later to open the new golf course.)

The small-town center was next to a harbor full of small fishing and sailing boats as well as one large sailing ship that was from Copenhagen. The young sailors from the sailing ship, in identical uniforms, were walking around town and going in and out of bars and restaurants. There is an old fortress on a hill called Fort Charlette that has a great view of the town. There were beautiful rolling green hills on the opposite side of the harbor. After walking around the center of town with many fine stone buildings as well as the fortress, I went over a hill where there is a miniature golf course. The course sits next to another bay where one can see the Atlantic Ocean and the North Atlantic Ocean meet.

The nights were short as the sun came out around four and set about ten. The next morning, I hired a taxi driver, Arthur, to take me to the airport the long way, through some small villages and by lots of farms. Most of the farms were surrounded by rock walls with lots of sheep (fourteen times the number of humans), some Shetland ponies, and a few cattle and horses grazing. There were many small abandoned stone homes, many with the roofs gone. Most of the homes in the villages and countryside were new and nice. The road was one lane in most places with turnoffs for passing. There were lots of rabbits crossing the roads.

After our arrival at the airport in Sumburgh, I caught a short Flybe airline flight to Orkney along with ten other passengers. The archipelago of Orkney is four miles from the mainland of Scotland. It has been inhabited for nine thousand years since the arrival of Mesolithic hunter-gather groups at the end of the Ice Age.

There were no taxis at the airport, so I caught a local bus into Kirkwall. The bus driver dropped me off near the hotel. After a five-minute walk, I arrived at the beautiful Lynnfield Hotel near the Highland Park distillery, a whiskey plant. The five-star hotel has ten exclusive rooms and was built in the 1800s. There were lots of old pictures on the walls and many antiques displayed. The rooms were all upstairs, and I had to walk up some squeaky old stairs to get to my room. There were no room numbers on the doors, only names. My room is called the Scarrataing. It is nice with a large bathtub that I enjoyed for two nights. The reception area adjoined a bar, lounge, and dining room. At dinner, I had to order in the lounge and was called to the dining room when the meal was ready.

Following check-in that morning, I left my backpack at the hotel and took a thirty-minute walk into town. I first went to the tourist office and found out that within half an hour, there was a three-hour bus tour of the important places on the island. So I signed up and paid for the trip. Neolithic Orkney is a UNESCO World Heritage site with a magical prehistoric landscape. On the tour, we drove by many farms with stone walls around the pastures containing mainly sheep, but also a few Shetland ponies and dairy cattle, just like in the Shetland Islands. I got to visit ancient civilization sites, such as the Ring of Brodgar (third-largest stone circle in the UK), Skara Brae (five-thousand-year-old Neolithic village), the seventeenth-century Skaill House (home of William Graham Watt, who discovered Skara Brae after a storm shifted the sand dunes in 1850), and the standing Stones of Stenness (the oldest stone circle on Orkney dating from around 3000 BC).

Following my return to Kirkwall, I exchanged some money at the post office (60 British pounds for $100) and then took a walk around the small downtown area next to the harbor. Like Lerwick, there were lots of fishing and sailing boats docked in the harbor. The buildings in the town were mainly stone, and the prominent two were the town hall, built in 1884, and St. Magnus Cathedral of Scotland, directly across the street from the town hall. The church had medieval architecture that took three hundred years to build. It is the most northerly cathedral in the British Isles. Next to the cathedral is the earl's and bishop's palace that is now a museum. There is a lot of damage to the building.

The next morning, I found out that 52 percent of the people in the UK had voted to leave the EU. I needed some more British pounds, so I returned to the post office to exchange $100, and I got 8 pounds more than I got the day before. Later, I took a ten-minute taxi ride to the Orkney Golf Club so I could play nine holes of golf. I rented clubs *and balls at the clubhouse, but there were no golf carts available, only a two-wheeled carrier. So I had to walk the whole two hours of play, where I only got up to seven holes and lost half-a-dozen balls. The good thing about the course that day was that there were only two other players there. I spent the rest of the day walking around town again.*

I checked out of the hotel the next morning and flew back to the U.S. via London. It had been a great trip.

Chapter 4
Troubles for Kim Carn

I

After John returned from his trip to Venezuela, he called Kim and told her that he had no luck in finding any of the information that she requested. She thanked him for his work and for making the cryptic phone call.

About a month later, Kim calls John from a pay phone in Atlanta. She starts to cry and tells him that her husband was killed by a hit-and-run driver in Kiev. "You are the only real friend I have, and I needed someone to talk to."

"What happened, Kim?"

"All the embassy could tell me is that they think Sidney's death was no accident as a speeding car came up on the sidewalk Sidney was walking on, ran over him, and fled. I agree with the ambassador's suspicions that Sidney was murdered as I had received a letter from him saying someone had ransacked his apartment, and he was worried about an attempt on his life. I plan to fly to Kiev tomorrow and make arrangements to have his body shipped to Washington for a quiet funeral."

Kim arrives in Kiev two days later to settle Sidney's affairs and to make arrangements to have his body shipped to Washington. She discovers his flat ransacked a second time. After Kim takes care of her husband's personal things, she joins several staff members for a brief memorial at the embassy. Later that day, Kim takes two suitcases to the curb and waits to hail a taxi to take her to the airport for her flight to the United States. As she is waiting for a taxi, a car comes down the street at high speed, jumps the curb, and just misses hitting her and her luggage. Then the car continues down the street at high speed.

Two weeks later, John gets another call from Kim. She tells him she is in Denver and would like to meet him in his apartment. Of course, he agrees. Kim arrives midafternoon and tells him that when she was in Kiev, a car almost hit her as she was waiting for a taxi to take her to the airport. "The car came up on the sidewalk, and I jumped out of the way as it sped by. I assume the driver was trying to kill me. After I returned to Atlanta following Sidney's funeral in Washington, I found that my apartment had been broken into and ransacked. I think whoever did that was looking for the papers Sidney sent me that incriminated the White House of trying to interfere with the next presidential election. As you know, the leading presidential candidate is the former American ambassador to the Ukraine. The White House wanted from the Ukraine government some damaging information about him in exchange for promised defense weapons. Sidney wrote that he obtained the information from a friend who was an assistant to the Uranian president. Sidney was warned by his boss not to disclose the information as it could not be substantiated.

"The man in the car could have been an assassin hired by a top CIA official on directions from the White House. One interesting thing that a former director of the CIA said during an interview in June 1962 was 'If the people ever find out what the CIA has done, we would be chased down in the streets and lynched.'

"Scarier, though, was what happened to me several days later. I went from my apartment on the tenth floor to the elevator on my way to work. Just as the elevator door was closing, a big scary-looking man slid into the elevator and stood behind me. A few seconds later, the giant put me in a bear hug and started to strangle me. Just before the elevator reached the ground floor, I fell to the floor unconscious. The next thing I knew was that a nice couple was attending me. Although I was shaken up, I told the couple that I was okay and thanked them for their help. They told me that when the elevator door opened, the evil man pushed them out of the way and ran from the building. They then moved me from of the elevator floor to the couch in the entryway.

"I then went to the office very shaken up and told my boss about the incident as well as the car almost hitting me in Kiev. He suggested I transfer to the Denver office since a position is available there. It took a couple of days to finish my work, give my landlord notice, and arrange to have my furniture and belongings shipped to Denver. I then loaded my car with clothes and personal things and took the two-day drive here. I am staying at the Brown Palace Hotel until I can find my own place."

With a friendly hug, John says, "I am so sorry to hear about your loss of Sidney and the attempts on your life. You are always welcome to stay with me."

"Thank you, dear friend. My first assignment here is to get information on a terrorist group arriving in several U.S. cities to disrupt our lives with simultaneous actions of putting poisonous substances in our water supplies and in public places to shut down hospitals and transportation systems. I received information that Colorado is one of the main targets because of the many government facilities located here that includes the North American Aerospace Defense Command in Colorado Springs.

"The CIA also received more specific information that terrorists had planned to steal some refined uranium to put in the drinking water of major cities. Usually, the water is not analyzed for uranium."

John tells Kim about his Clemson student project of removing arsenic and uranium from drinking water for an environmental contest held each year at New Mexico State University. "My student's project was based on an actual incident in a South Carolina town. After numerous people got cancer, the authorities traced it to the town's drinking water. Further investigation revealed deposits of uranium ore in the same underground locations as the town's well water.

"One possible source of radioactive material is a uranium ore processing facility near Grand Junction. There has been a big problem with radioactive radon gas in some of the new homes built over uranium tailings from the ore processing. I suggest we visit this facility and find out what type of safeguards they have in preventing the stealing of processed uranium. We could fly there and rent a car or just drive. If we drove, you could see more of the beauty of Colorado."

"That sounds like an excellent idea, John. Let me tell my supervisor about your suggestion and see if he agrees with your plan."

"Would you like to have dinner with me at the Brown Palace? We could meet in the restaurant at six."

"That sounds wonderful, John. Now I need to return to work since I have a meeting to attend."

That evening, as the two are having dinner, Kim tells John that her boss has approved the trip to Grand Junction. "When would you like to go, John?"

"Why don't we leave next Monday in my car so I can show you some of the beauty of Colorado. We could stay in Glenwood Springs on Monday night and arrive in Grand Junction before noon on Tuesday for an afternoon visit to the uranium facility. I will contact the plant manager and arrange the meeting."

"Okay. Can you pick me up at six on Monday morning at the Brown Palace?"

"Certainly. But first, can you meet me for lunch tomorrow so I can discuss more of the details of the trip? I should also know if the plant manager is available for our visit on Tuesday afternoon. We could meet at the Civic Center Park at noon and buy lunch at one of the kiosks."

"That sounds great, John, and thank you for dinner. By the way, could I borrow another one of your travel diaries to read about some of your great trips? The stories are so interesting and educational."

"Thank you for your kind words. I will bring one to our meeting tomorrow at noon. Good night."

II

John arrives in the park and spies Kim sitting alone at a park bench. He joins her, and she thanks him for bringing one of his diaries to read. "You are welcome to borrow more of my diaries if you wish to read about a few more of my trips. I would also recommend reading *The Bare Essentials*, a book Margrit wrote. Here is a free copy for you. The story involves a University of Colorado chemistry professor who goes to the University of Vienna for a year's sabbatical. His friend, who is head of the analytical laboratory of Warsaw's Nuclear Energy Institute, asks him to analyze samples of natural gas to see if the gas contains mind-altering drugs. He suspects that the drugs are being introduced by the Russians to subdue the Polish people during the Cold War. The professor agrees to perform the analysis but is unaware that by doing so, he will subject both himself and his Polish-born wife to acts of terror, including an attempt on his life.

"By the way, I have been invited to attend a dinner with my family at Eric and Sylvia's home in Boulder on Saturday. Would you like to join me? Please say yes as it may help you get your mind off the tragic events you have experienced recently. All of my family will be there, and it would be a good time for you to meet them. I will just introduce you as a friend I met at Clemson and not mention the CIA. You can say that you have a government job at the Federal Building in Denver and have just been transferred here from Atlanta. I can pick you up at the Brown Palace at one so we can have a drive around Boulder, and I can show you CU. It's funny that the initials are just like Clemson University."

After a short walk on the Pearl Street Mall in Downtown Boulder and at the CU campus on Saturday afternoon, John and Kim travel to Eric and Sylvia's home in South Boulder for dinner. Amy, Dave, and Lorrie arrive, and the five young adults spend some time exchanging information with Kim over a wonderful meal that Sylvia has prepared. There is also a discussion of everyone's recent activities. Eric explains to Kim about his job working for a biotech company in nearby Longmont and how he and Sylvia met. "My wonderful wife works at the same company I do, and we met at CU. We bought this house last year after we were married. We know the house is small with only two bedrooms, but housing is expensive in Boulder, and this is all we could afford. I plan on finishing the basement sometime in the future. Prior to the home purchase, we were living in separate condos and before that in dorm rooms at CU, finishing our doctorate degrees, mine in organic chemistry and Sylvia's in biochemistry."

John brags about Eric. "One of Eric's goals is to climb all the mountains in Colorado above fourteen thousand feet. Eric, I think you have climbed about half of them, right?"

"Yes, Dad, twenty-eight of them."

Amy speaks up next. "After graduating from the American International School in Vienna, I returned to Colorado and started working for an investment company in Downtown Denver. There, I met Dave, who worked in a separate department. After a year of courtship, we were married and purchased a home in Aurora. Okay Lorrie, what do you have to say?"

"Thank you, Amy. I just started graduate school, majoring in organic chemistry. As you can guess, my father was a big influence on Eric and my studies. I have been staying with Eric and Sylvia."

Lorrie thanks her father for bringing one of his diaries that has the story of his last trip to the South Pacific. She says that she would like to take a trip there someday.

After dinner, John and Kim thank their hosts for a wonderful time and return to Denver.

The flight from Los Angeles was late in landing in Tahiti, and I almost missed my connection to Atuona, Hiva Oa, in the Marquesas Islands. The Air Tahiti plane was a small two-engine turbo. After about four hours, the plane made an hour's stop in Nuku Hiva, a beautiful island. The flight from Tahiti only had about a dozen passengers, but in leaving Nuku Hiva for Hiva Oa, it was full, about fifty passengers.

I was picked up at the small two-gate Hiva Oa airport by Michael. He is serving as an intern at the beautiful Hiva Oa Hanakee Pearl Lodge (three stars). Michael is working on a master's degree in hotel management in France. The ride from the airport to the hotel was twenty minutes. My hotel room is a small hut with a covered front porch, and there are fourteen other traditional Polynesian bungalows at the hotel. It is perched high on the hillside above the bay of Atuona overlooking the ocean and mountains, including Mt. Ootuna, about 2,800 feet in elevation. The beautiful mountains are covered in a variety of trees, including palm and evergreens. The hotel restaurant overlooks the swimming pool. There are lots of chickens running around the hotel grounds, and one even came into the dining room where I was having lunch. Following lunch, the hotel driver took me to the small village of Nukuttiva. There, I exchanged $200 for 2,000 francs CFP of the Republic of France. I had a walk around the village that only took thirty minutes. After buying some water and a visit to the post office, the hotel driver came and took me back to the hotel.

Following breakfast the next morning, I was picked up for an all-day guided tour of the eastern half of the island. (Atuona is south of the airport, which is near the middle of the island.) We went to Eiaone, Puamau, and Hana Hehe, the other three main villages on the island. West of Atuona is the highest mountain, Mount Temetin (3,800 feet). Puamau is on the northeast tip of Hiva Oa. It was a breathtaking drive along the winding coastline through several valleys. We visited Te Iipona, an archaeological site containing Takai, the tallest stone tiki of French Polynesia (730 feet), and the very exceptional Makaii Taua Pepe, a unique tiki represented horizontally. Lunch was at the Marquesas

House, along with eight to nine cats. It was a nice lunch of wild pig and goat, raw fish, rice, and coconut. I was popular with the cats as I gave them my raw fish and tough meat.

On the way to Puamau, we made a stop at Pualei and a village on the sea, Hanumate. After seeing Puamau, we stopped in an area for swimming. Fellow passengers, Kayla and Py, and Henry (Heimata), our driver and guide, who spoke good English and French, went for an hour's swim. I had a walk and visited a nearby church in the village. Some information about my traveling companions: Henry grew up on the island and has a wife and a two-year-old daughter. He says she (his daughter) is "fresh," ha ha. Kayla is an American from a small town in Montana. Her mother was born in Korea. Kayla does look (her eyes) like she is half Korean. At first, I thought she was part American Indian like a good friend of mine. Py is French. They met at the French plant of Dow Chemical, and now they both work for Dow Chemical in Hanover. They spent nine months in China, so we had a lot to talk about. Both are about thirty with master's degrees in chemical engineering and are a nice-looking couple.

On the drive, most roads are curvy and covered in gravel. Near and in villages, the streets were concrete. From the hotel to the airport, the road is asphalt. We stopped at the airport on the way back, and it was open with no one there. Tomorrow we go in the opposite direction for about two hours prior to my 1:00 p.m. flight to Tahiti.

The next morning, we visited Taaoa Valley via the southern coast road and saw the archaeological site called Upeke, one of the largest ceremonial places of French Polynesia. It occupies most of the valley and contains ancient residential platforms, tiki, and altars of sacrifice. We also went to Taaoa village and saw a nice Catholic church. Dany, my driver today, spoke little English and drove slowly

compared with yesterday's driver. The big guy also asked a
lot of times if he should stop for pictures, unlike Henry.

Last night and the night before, I could see at least a
thousand stars, including the Southern Cross. The evenings
were cool, but it was hot and humid during the day. In the
afternoon, I caught my Air Tahiti flight at one and arrived
three hours later. I was sitting next to a young beautiful
Tahitian lady. She said she was a midwife, and I asked her
how many children she took care of. She said thirty. Wow.
I asked, "What ages?" She said twenty to thirty. Now I
wondered if they were adults and not children.

After a two-hour wait in Tahiti, I caught my delayed
flight to Bora Bora. I had the window seat in the first row,
and the sun was just setting. Doug, the gentleman on the
aisle seat, was interesting. He had grown up in Hawaii
(his father a civil engineer), started out at a college in
Pennsylvania, but did not like it and moved to Townsville,
Australia, to get his degree in marine biology. Now he works
for the French Polynesian government visiting all the islands
to collect information on the needs of the residents. He gave
up his U.S. citizenship because he did not want to pay U.S.
income taxes. In French Polynesia, there is no income tax,
only 30 percent sales tax on everything. By the way, I was
amazed that there was no security check in Atuona, only in
Tahiti. The Tahiti airport is not too big and has only three
domestic gates.

Bora Bora is located 170 miles northwest of Tahiti and
is a small island that covers only 23 square miles. It is part
of a small basaltic chain whose tallest point is Mt. Otemanu,
with a height of 2,200 feet. Bora Bora was formed after
many volcanic eruptions that began four million years ago
and continued over hundreds of thousands of years. Since
then, the island has undergone a slow sinking movement. Its
lagoon is encircled by a wide coral reef that encloses several
big motus or small islands with white sand beaches and

*luxury resorts. Its population is about nine thousand with
a consistent temperature about eighty degrees Fahrenheit.*

*The first Polynesians arrived in Bora Bora around 900
AD, shortly having settled on the island of Raiatea. According
to Polynesian mythology, Bora Bora (or Pora Pora), which
stands for "first born," was the first island drawn out of the
ocean after the creation of Havai'l (Raiatea). The people
of Bora Bora were converted to Protestantism, and their
church was organized by the reverend John Orsmond in
1818. The way of life for Bora Bora's population remained
traditional all during the nineteenth century, not much
disturbed by the development of the two export crops of
copra and vanilla. Operation Bobcat brought five thousand
American soldiers to the island in December 1942. A 6,562-
foot aviation runway was built, eight artillery guns were
installed, and thirty fuel storage facilities were built. But
the retreat of the Japanese left Bora Bora free from combat,
and the Americans exited the island in June 1946.*

*Upon landing in Bora Bora, it seemed like the whole
island was lit up with homes on each side of the road circling
the big island as well as all the homes and huts on the
sandbars. The airport is on a small island not connected to
the main island, so I had to take a water taxi to the main
island where the expensive Hotel Sofitel is located. The next
day, Saturday, October 29, I took a taxi a short ways into the
main village of Vaitape. I had a walk in the heat. The village
is only about four to five blocks long, with supermarket,
bank, and many shops selling pearls. The only restaurant
was closed, so I had an ice cream bar and soda instead
of a nice lunch. In the bay, there were several small boats
and one large cruise ship anchored. Nearby was a beautiful
church. Surprisingly, so far, everywhere I went in French
Polynesia, I saw Halloween decorations.*

*In the afternoon, I joined a newlywed couple from
California and an old Australian for a slow ride around the*

island (twenty-four miles). Our driver/guide was Joshua, a big Polynesian who had grown up on Bora Bora and spoke excellent English. He drove a Land Cruiser 4-wheeler, and it was needed in two places since we drove up steep hills on rocky roads to get outstanding views of the nearby blue and green waters. We also had a nice view of the bungalows that were built on the reefs that surround most of the main island. On the way back going through Vaitape, there was a wedding taking place.

On Sunday, I had an unwanted cold shower since there was no hot water at the hotel. After breakfast, I wrote postcards and brought my diary up to date. I caught the hotel's water taxi in the late afternoon for a ride to the airport for my evening flight to Papeete. I thought Bora Bora was boring but beautiful. I did not need a second day there. It would have been much different if I would have had my family with me. It is a great place for newlyweds. On the water taxi to the airport, I met a nice couple from Boulder, small world. The gentleman grew up in Boulder and is an attorney. The lady is a housewife. They have three boys, twelve, fourteen, and sixteen.

I stayed at the Tahiti Pearl Beach Resort that evening. It is quite a fancy hotel, four stars, and expensive. It is a pity I did not have time to enjoy the big whirlpool in my big hotel room. I did have dinner at the hotel restaurant next to the beach and ocean.

I got up the next morning, October 31, at five and took a taxi to the airport. I am flying Air Tahiti to Auckland, and we lose a day, arriving on November 1, after a six-hour flight on an Airbus A340. I missed Halloween evening, my favorite holiday. I blame it on the International Date Line. So far, all the airports in French Polynesia, including Papeete, used the runway for takeoffs, landings, and taxing.

At the departure gate for my flight to Nouméa, I found out they had no reservation for me, and the plane was full.

I then went to the Air New Zealand desk and got a seat on the morning flight. In addition, I got vouchers for dinner and lunch and a room at the plush Novotel directly across from the international terminal. It took me three minutes to walk there and check in. I had turned (or was it my guardian angels) a bad situation into something nice as there was a bus nearby that took me into the city for a walkabout. The city reminded me of Adelaide as there was a free bus that took me around the city center, an area about five by ten blocks. One interesting sight was a young man playing beautiful music with drumsticks and a variety of pots, small trash cans, and other containers. The city even has a space needle like in Sydney and Seattle. The Aotea Square, next to the town hall, was especially nice. My visit was very pleasant. Later, I caught the bus back to the hotel, where I had a free dinner.

On November second, I left the hotel and walked across the street for my flight check-in. After immigration and a security check (no removal of shoes or bag of liquids), I went to the Air New Zealand club room for more food and drink while I waited for boarding. I had seat 3C. The flight to New Caledonia was three hours. There is a two-hour time difference, so I had gained two hours. It is in the same time zone as Sydney. The Air New Zealand flight had a very funny safety video, and I watched the entertaining and funny movie The Campaign. *It was similar to the presidential campaign that will end in a week. Will Farrell starred in the movie. The airport in New Caledonia is nice and new, and I exchanged $100 for 9,065 XPF (Pacific francs). The country is French-speaking, and the natives are a mix of African and Polynesian appearing people. The island is 420 miles long and has a population of 276,000 residents.*

The airport is about 25 miles from Nouméa, and I took a hotel bus to the three-star Nouvata Hotel. The ride went through a beautiful mountain range covered with numerous types of vegetation, tropical trees, and evergreens. The land appeared to be dry in places, and a mountain in the distance appeared to have had a forest fire on it. There were lots of ranches with cattle. Nouméa is very touristic with beautiful beaches and several small shopping malls with mostly two to four story buildings. There is a beautiful big church as well as a smaller church in the small city center. The bus went through the city to the other side, where the hotel is located.

After I checked into the hotel, I took a fifteen-minute public bus ride into the center of the city. There was a nice park at the end of the bus line with a statue. In the park were groups of women talking. I went back to the hotel after about a two-hour walk about the city. Then I took a walk near the hotel and on the beach.

I made an early night of it since I had to get up early the next morning to catch the bus at five to the airport. The flight to Sydney left at eight and arrived three hours later. I had a four-hour wait for the Air New Zealand flight to Christchurch, but it went easier for me as I spent most of that time in the nice airline lounge with very few people there. I watched CNN, got caught up with this diary, and edited my recent photos. I arrived late in Christchurch and got a taxi for a fifteen-minute drive to the Ashley Hotel. I hate to say the hotel was more like a motel.

I had to get up at five the next morning to catch my six o'clock flight to Dunedin (pronounced daa-needen). I was surprised that there was no security check at the airport. On the small plane prior to takeoff, a couple of passengers nearby were giving me a bad look. The stewardess came by and asked me to turn my alarm clock off that was in my pocket. I did not hear it, but it turned out the battery was dying and was calling out for help. The stewardess took my small alarm clock back into the galley so it would not bother the passengers around me. The flight was only an hour, and there was a beautiful snow-capped mountain range to the west and the ocean to the east with the sun. As the plane neared our destination, the mountains were replaced by beautiful hills covered with grass. There were periodic brown patches that I would find out later were fields of pesky weeds that the farmers had to work hard in removing. Most of the farms had grazing cattle and sheep.

The airport was small and used the runway for taxing. There was a ramp to walk off the plane on, no stairs. I took a thirty-minute shuttle ride into the city for $30 NZ. I checked in early at the Wains Hotel in the city center. The hotel was old but had been renovated. After breakfast at McDonald's and a two-hour walk, I took a wonderful three-hour bus tour to see the Larnach Castle and to have a tour of the city. The castle is twenty minutes from Central Dunedin near the village of Portabella and the bay. It is on a large peninsula.

I was at the castle about two hours for a walk around the beautiful gardens, a tour of the castle, and lunch.

The castle has quite an interesting history. William Larnach was a successful landowner, Minister of the Crown, banker, financier, and merchant baron. His lasting legacy is his great castle overlooking the spectacular Otago Harbour. Larnach built the castle for his beloved first wife, Eliza Jane Guise. Construction began in 1871, and two hundred workmen labored for three years before the family moved in. Skilled European craftsmen worked for twelve more years to embellish the interior with the finest materials from around the world. Building was completed with the addition of a splendid ballroom in 1887. Our guide said it is the only castle in New Zealand. Later in life, Larnach had some personal problems that are not fully known today. Because of this situation, he took his own life with a single pistol shot to the head while he was seated alone in a committee room in Parliament, thus died one of the New Zealand's most remarkable men.

Some of the things I saw from the bus, and later on my walk, were St. Paul's Cathedral, the First Church of Otago; St. Joseph's Cathedral; hilltop viewpoints of the city, harbor, and surrounding green hills; Baldwin Street (the steepest in the world); botanic gardens; University of Otago (with twenty thousand students); Dunedin Stadium; and the magnificent and historic railway station.

After my walk in the city, I went to the bank and got $124 NZ for $100. I then went to Speight's Brewery for dinner. I read the Otago Daily Times *after I got to my room. On the front page was a report that the government had awarded Otago University a research grant of $65 million. The universities of Auckland, Victoria, and Canterbury each got twenty-one, fourteen, and five million, respectively. On the second page of the* Times *was a short article about the cruise ship* Sea Princess *docking with two thousand passengers. It came from Akaroe and will sail for Fjordland the next day. Also reported was that the ice-hardened ship* Italica *was set to go to Antarctica with supplies for the Italian base there.*

By the way, Dunedin has a population of 110,000 and is the oldest city in New Zealand. It is touted as New Zealand's most beautiful city and home of the rare yellow-eyed penguin on the Otago Peninsula. It also has the only mainland breeding colony of the royal albatross. Dunedin is New Zealand's second-largest city by area and has the finest example of Victorian and Edwardian architecture in the southern hemisphere—one thing I loved. In fact, I now think I will move here instead of Vancouver, Canada, if Trump is elected president. Almost everyone I spoke with did not want him elected for various reasons, including the effect he would have on their country.

The next day, I went on a train trip through the Taieri River Gorge west of Dunedin giving views of Dunedin city, Taieri Plain, and the Gorge that can be seen only by train. The Gorge is full of dark peaty pools, white water rapids, sheer cliffs, towering via ducts, and ten train tunnels.

Before the train went through the canyon with river, it passed many farms with sheep, cows, and horses. The area is beautiful with green hills. On the trip, I got acquainted with two young Japanese girls. They are studying tourism at a university in Wellington. They spoke excellent English and were good-looking.

That evening, I had a small Greek salad at an outdoor restaurant in the center of the city where the town hall and a large church are located. There were lots of college students at the restaurants in the area, and others were walking about carrying open beer bottles. Earlier I had stopped by the Cadbury manufacturing plant and bought a milk chocolate bar. Someone mentioned that the winters are very mild, and some years they get a dusting of snow (just like in South Carolina). The area around Dunedin reminded me of Scotland.

The next day, I left Dunedin at 1:05 p.m. for a one-hour flight to Christchurch on a Virgin Australia flight. I had about a four-and-a-half-hour wait in the New Zealand lounge for my three-and-a-half-hour flight to Sydney, again on Virgin. There was a security check in Christchurch but not at the nice four-gate Dunedin airport.

Early on Monday, November 7, after a good night at the Sydney Travelodge Hotel near Museum Station, I took the 373 bus to Coogee Bay for a look at the nice seaside. Later, I caught the bus to Randwick Junction, where I exchanged money and had a walk to see my former residences where Margrit and I lived for three years. Then I walked through the university campus to the chemical engineering building, where I used to work. At the administration desk, a lady told me that they have a new head of school and that a friend had left to join another university. Next door is the new chemistry building that is named after another old friend who was head of the department. As I saw during my last visit, it appeared like most of the students are Asian.

Later, I caught the bus to Circular Quay, where I had quick lunch. Then I took a ferry ride to Watson Bay, followed by another ferry ride in the opposite direction to Parramatta. There were fourteen stops on the way that included Darling Harbor, Cockatoo Island, Kissing Point, and Sydney Olympic Park, where the Parramatta River started getting narrower, about a block wide. There were lots of new homes along the way as well as different sizes of sailing boats anchored. The weather was super, short-sleeve shirt and blue skies. It was my first time on this ferry. By the way, only the Opal card (it looks like a credit card) can be used for paying the bus, ferry, and train rides now, no cash or tickets.

My next adventure was taking the new light rail (the only one in Sydney) from Central Station to the end stop. There were about a dozen stops. Next, I went back to Circular Quay, where I caught the ferry to Manley. There, I had a walk to the beach. Later, I returned to Circular Quay, where I took a bus ride to Botany, then a walk around Chinatown. After a Big Mac meal, I made an early night of it since my flight to Perth left at seven the next morning.

The flight to Perth was five hours, and I watched a couple of good movies. The time change was a gain of three hours. My Virgin Airlines flight for Onslow left Perth at 1:45 p.m. The two-hour plane ride was over a very desolate desert with lots of red earth and no water. As the plane descended into Onslow, I could see numerous salt islands where salt is harvested from the ocean using solar evaporation. (It is one of the main industries here besides oil and gas production.) In 2004, Chevron Australia discovered the Wheatstone offshore gas resource about 120 miles north of Onslow.

They decided to transport the gas to a domestic liquefied gas plant near Onslow. The name Wheatstone comes from the Wheatstone Channel in the Montebello Islands, an archipelago of 174 small islands, 80 miles off the Pilbara coast and 60 miles south of the gas field. The plant employs seven thousand workers that live in company apartments near the plant. The company pays for their board and room as well as flights to their homes, mainly in Perth, every four weeks so they can have a week at home. They work twelve-hour days.

The Onslow airport is small (one gate) as is the town (seven hundred people). I was lucky again as the only taxi in town arrived, and another passenger got in first. It turned out the gentleman was born in South Africa and moved here as a young man. He is now a sales representative for Chevron. Our Chinese driver, Emily, drove us to the Beadon Bay Hotel, and my new friend paid for the taxi ride. An English lady, Lorretta, checked us in and gave me a nice room on the third floor overlooking the Indian Ocean. That evening, after I had a walkabout and dinner, I watched the news about the election of Trump. He said the world is going to have a wild ride the next four years.

That evening, the wind was blowing red dirt around, but the weather the next morning was much better with calm winds, blue skies, and a good temperature. After breakfast, I took an hour's drive around the town in Emily's taxi. She and her Australian husband also have a cleaning service. Emily also drove out near the salt and gas/oil production areas. The suburban housing is nice with a typical home in the $300,000 to $400,000 range. There is a new subdivision going up, and one school serves all grades (1–12).

Only a few tourists are here as the season ended and the cyclone season started. Years ago, a cyclone destroyed the original town of Onslow, and the new town was built farther northeast to Beadon Bay. At 1:00 p.m., a friend of

Emily came in his four-wheel drive Toyota Land Cruiser and took me out to the old city, about a twelve-mile ride. There is a termite town about six miles from Onslow, home of the spinifex termite; they are grass feeders and do not attack timber. We also passed the new gas and oil plant that Chevron is building with Bechtel as the contractor. The area is covered in various types of vegetation, including grass. Near the Ashburton River, there were many cattle grazing. On the second half of the trip, we went from a nice asphalt highway to a one-lane dirt road. At the end of the road is the site of old Onslow. Only the walls of the jail and courthouse remain. The town was proclaimed in 1883 and named after Alexander Onslow, who was the chief justice of Western Australia at the time. The town was on the banks of the Ashburton River and served the pearling, mining, and pastoral industries until the 1920s, when it was moved to Beadon Bay. The new town hosted the allied navy in World War II and was the wrath of Japanese bombers in 1943.

After the tour, I had another walk. The beaches in Onslow are nice, but one needs to watch out for saltwater crocodiles. The lady at the visitor's center also warned me to look out for wild cats and dogs (dogs cross bred by Dingos) if I go on a bush walk. The sea is good for several kinds of fish and crab. On the walk, I had a look at the war memorial northwest of Onslow's town edge. A nice boardwalk starts there and continues parallel to the beach all the way to the cargo ship pier. I did not make it all the way there because of all the pesky flies attacking me. Later, after returning to town, I took a walk to the store and played a game of pool in the hotel bar by myself.

Friday was a very boring day for me as there was nothing I could do. The ferry to the island was not operating, and it seemed like I was the only tourist in town. I took a two-block walk to the store, and few people were about. I mainly took a nap and watched TV until three when Emily drove me to the small airport. The two-hour flight to Perth left at 5:20 p.m. In Perth, I had a wait of five hours for my five-hour Jet Star flight to Singapore. There, I had another two-hour wait for the SilkAir flight to Medan. I stayed at the Santika Premiere Dyandra Hotel and Convention Center after my arrival in Medan at 8:00 a.m.

Medan is in North Sumatra and is a culinary mecca, big and interesting, and about an hour's drive from the nice and big airport. I exchanged money at the bank following my arrival from the airport, $1 = 13,000 rupiah. No coins are used, only 2,000, 5,000, 10,000, 20,000, 50,000, and 100,000 Ribu rupiah notes. The hotel is five stars and nice. My room is on the twelfth floor with a great view of half of the sprawling city of three million people. There are a large variety of buildings in the city, some old, some very nice, and a few new skyscrapers. Traffic is terrible with lots of cars, motorcycles, and Bek Bekas (a two-person carriage hooked to a motorcycle).

I had a walk near the hotel and found that some streets do not have sidewalks, and the ones with sidewalks had big gaps in them for water runoff. There is a big park across from the hotel where a police festival was being held with lots of people, a band, and speeches. A wedding was taking place at the hotel, and there were lots of people there but no Caucasians. I think I am the only tourist in town, just like in Onslow. Everyone here seems very friendly with a hello and smile. I assumed that most people looking at me, judging by the expression on their faces, think I am from another planet. One group of young ladies, after saying hello and where are you from, said, "Your hair looks just like Trump's." At that point, I puffed up my lips and put on a scowling look as to look more like the Donald. The city has at least one McDonald's, KFC, Pizza Hut, and A&W. There are many mosques and Christian churches in the city as well as one *large university. So far, the weather has been nice, short-sleeve shirt and blue skies.*

Back in my room, I watched the news. The major stories were about a 7.4 earthquake near Christchurch (I was just there five days ago), an earthquake about a week ago in Japan, Europe getting a lot of snow, and high winds in Brisbane. I checked my email before bedtime and received some terrible news that a boyhood friend had passed a couple of days earlier because of breathing problems. He had been in and out of hospitals most of the year, and the doctors could not find the cause. Bill and I were friends since seventh grade, and we both had chemistry labs in our backyards.

On Sunday morning, Syahrial picked me up for a seven-hour, seventy-mile drive (in a nice Toyota van) to see Lake Toba, the world's largest volcanic lake (caldera). There is also the beautiful Sipiso-piso waterfall nearby, which is fifteen feet wide and six hundred feet high, that feeds the lake. Traffic was not too bad leaving the city as Sundays are bike days. After leaving the major metropolis area, we went through numerous towns that mainly line the two-lane highway. On the way there was a smoking volcano in the distance (Mt. Iselate). The road got very curvy as we went over a beautiful mountain range completely covered by jungle.

High above the lake is an outstanding lookout with souvenir shops and a restaurant. One could see the giant lake in one direction and the spectacular waterfall in the other direction. There are steps that lead to the bottom of the falls, but Syahrial told me it would take forty minutes. My feet were in no shape for the walk, and we proceeded by car down the mountain on a very curvy and narrow paved road to the lake, where there is a nice small village. On the way back, lots of crazy drivers were passing us around curves on the highway packed with buses, cars, and motorcycles, even *a few brave souls on bikes. There were lots of orchards and farms along the way as well as roadside stalls selling fruit and vegetables. The main thing I saw were lots of oranges and even a troop of monkeys. There were many dogs in the villages and towns as well as chickens running around. We stopped at one traditional village and had a short walk to see the old types of homes. We got to go inside one, and it was interesting that there was an open fire on the floor where an old lady was cooking food. Syahrial only charged me $65 for the trip that I really enjoyed.*

Syahrial picked me up at six the next morning. The ride to the airport was almost an hour, even though traffic was light. The Medan airport is fairly large with twelve gates. There was light rain as I left Medan on the SilkAir Flight to Singapore. The flight was very bumpy, and the landing in the rain was scary.

At the airport, I exchanged $100 for 140 Singapore dollars. I stayed at the nice Village Hotel Bugis in the center of the city. It continued to rain in Singapore, and the hop-on, hop-off bus tour in the afternoon made picture taking not so good as I could not ride in the open upper part of the bus. Some of the bus stops were Little India, City Hall, Supreme Court, Boat Quay, Chinatown, and the Old Customs House. The main stops on the Yellow Bus that I took later were Clarke Quay, Botanic Garden, Raffles City, and Suntec Hub.

Singapore is a big, clean, and nice city with lots of skyscrapers and some buildings with unique architecture. There are also blocks of old two-story stores that are attractive. The Sultan's Mosque is across from the Village Hotel, and I had an excellent view of it from my fourteenth-story room. There were blue skies the second morning, and I repeated the two bus tours and also saw Universal Studios, a nice zoo, the Botanical Gardens, and several big shopping malls under major hotels, including the Bugis.

That evening, I met one of my former students who is now a professor at the university. We had dinner at Margareta's, a Mexican food restaurant, and talked about our days in New South Wales when he and his wife were my graduate students. They live in an apartment in Singapore. That evening, there was a super full moon that does not occur but every few years.

The next morning, I left the hotel at six in a driving rainstorm for the airport. I walked around the big Singapore airport (a fourth terminal is being built) after having breakfast at McDonald's. The plane flew out at nine in light rain. The SilkAir flight (three and a half hours to Davao) was full, 190 passengers, in a Boeing 737. The plane landed in Davao at one, and I took a taxi to the Crown Regency Residences. Davao is a large city area wise with a population of about 1.8 million. I got 4,750 Philippine peso for $100 and found that services and food are very inexpensive. For example, the forty-five-minute taxi ride from the good-sized Davao airport to the hotel was only $10. Breakfasts were only $5.

I went to the Eden Nature Park with Arnold, my hired driver. On the drive, we first drove through two small villages, Intal town and Calinan town. During the ride, Arnold told me a few things about himself and his country. He has three daughters, most people speak English as well as their native tongue (English is taught in grade school, and everywhere the signs are in English), and there are two main seasons in the country, hot and hotter. However, that afternoon, we drove back in a light rain shower.

The nature park is also a tourist camp, with many small cabins. There is a restaurant, café, and a three-mile nature hike on which I went part way. There is also a bird sanctuary and a big pen with four black deer. Next, we went to Jack's Ridge, where there is a restaurant and lookout over the entire city to the ocean. The city is surrounded by ocean on one side and a beautiful mountain range with jungle on the other side. We then went to the crocodile park, bone museum, and eagle sanctuary. The tour concluded with a drive around the city center with hundreds of cars, buses, and motorcycles. Traffic was terrible. The small buses hold about a dozen passengers with four places to hang on outside. We went by the town hall, several high-rise hotels, some nice churches, a big university, hospital, and several grade schools as well as several large modern shopping centers. Arnold told me that their president Duterte was born in Davao.

Following the tour, Arnold took me back to the hotel, which was not the best so far on this trip (big problem was that it was very noisy with only single-pane windows and lots of noisy people outside). On my last night in the hotel, the hotel clerk told me that the hotel and others in the city were fully booked because of a chain store convention of some type. The next morning the major news stories were that the Philippines had a 7 percent growth in their economy during the last quarter, the highest in Asia; a university professor was awarded an IR-100 award in Washington, D.C. (I had received two of the awards while I was at Rocky Flats), and the Miss Universe contest will be held in the Philippines next year. There are at least two McDonald's, KFCs, and Pizza Huts in the city.

On Friday, November 18, I took a short walk near the hotel and spent some time at the Iglesia ni Cristo church, which is a beautiful white church. Across the street is the Cosmopolitan Memorial Chapel. My walk was short since there were many places next to the street that had no sidewalks and where cars were parked. At 10:30 a.m., Arnold arrived and took me to the airport for my five-hour SilkAir flight to Singapore that arrived at 7:00 p.m. The flight to Singapore had a short stop in Cebu, where everyone had to deplane. Cebu is on a separate island, one of the four major ones. The fourth one has the main city of Kalibo. The Cebu airport is nice and of good size. There were flights to Dubai, Tokyo, Seoul, and several other international cities. On takeoff, I saw many small islands surrounded by green waters, with some of them having clusters of homes. I was told there are about one thousand islands in the Philippines.

At the Singapore airport, I had to wait until one o'clock, Saturday morning, for my five-hour China Eastern flight to Shanghai. On the flight from Singapore to Shanghai, I sat next to a Chinese couple. The guy said he was a mechanical engineer, and I wanted to tell him my mechanical engineer's joke. His wife spoke much better English than her husband, and she said he would not understand the story, and besides that, he is really a car mechanic. After a three-hour wait in Shanghai, I caught another China Eastern flight to Okinawa. This flight was only two hours, and I had an interesting companion on the flight. She was a young good-looking Japanese lady who had just spent a week in Paris and was flying back via Dubai and Shanghai. She works in a manufacturing plant.

This was an extremely tiring trip for me that was almost twenty-four hours. The only thing that helped me at the Singapore and Shanghai airports were their airplane lounges where I waited for my flights.

After landing at the Naha Airport, I exchanged $100 for 10,700 JPY. There was a young girl, about four or five, at the bank playing with the magnetic numbers that showed various exchange rates. I was hoping she would make the U.S. Dollar stronger. I then caught a public bus, and after about a half-hour ride, I arrived at a large shopping mall after going by an A&W, KFC, and 7-Eleven. After exiting from the bus, I had a walkabout at the big and nice mall and then caught a taxi to the nice and modern Grand Mer Resort. I am staying on the eighth floor of the fourteen-story building. From the balcony, there is a nice view to the *west overlooking the bay and harbor. That evening, I had dinner in the room.*

After breakfast Sunday morning, my driver/guide, Tachi, picked me up for a four-hour drive south to Sefa-Utaki, Okinawa World Culture Kingdom/Gyokusendo Caves, and the Shurijo Castle Park. I paid 12,000 JPY for the trip. Unfortunately, Tachi did not speak English, but he did guide me through all three places.

The drive to Sefa-Utaki was along the sea on HY-329 to HY-331. After we arrived at Sefa-Utaki, Tachi and I had about a half-mile walk on a trail going down to beautiful rock formations and a big rock arch. This was the most sacred site of the Ryukyu Kingdom. I really got a workout on the walk. Next, we had a drive to the Gyokusendo Caves. It is one of the largest cave systems in Japan with an overall length of three miles, with over a million stalactites. At the end of the tunnel, we exited through a long shopping area with crafts, Nanto Brewery, and a tropical orchard. We were in Yaese Towa.

Finally, we traveled back toward Naha City, where the Shurijo Castle Park is located, a World Heritage site. It is said that Shurijo Castle was constructed around the fourteenth century; however, the details are not known. Since becoming the royal seat in 1406 for King Sho Hashi, who united the kingdom, the castle proudly served as the heart of the politics, foreign diplomacy, and culture of the Ryukyu Kingdom for approximately five hundred years until King Sho Tai, the last ruler of the kingdom, abdicated the throne to the Meiji government. Through trade with China, Japan, and Southeast Asia, various items were brought to Shurijo Castle, where the distinct culture of Ryukyu blossomed through the arts, such as lacquer ware, dyes, textiles, ceramics, and music. The Seiden of Shurijo Castle was reduced to dust during the Okinawa War of 1945. In the commemoration of the twentieth anniversary of homeland return of Okinawa, it was restored in 1992 with eighteenth-century Shurijo as the model. On the way back, we went through Ginowan City to Okinawa City, where the Grand Mer Resort is located. The whole island is called Okinawa, and Naha City is the capital and is where the airport is located.

At the resort, I only saw six to eight Caucasians. One of the resort desk clerks was a young American who was there as a dependent of his father stationed here in the army. That evening, I went to the American Café on the eighth floor so I could look at the menu. I was not that hungry and only had a soda. When I went to pay for the soda, the young bartender gave me a dart and told me if I hit the bull's-eye on the dartboard, the soda would be free. Otherwise, whatever number I hit, he would give me a percent off the bill. I did get 10 percent reduction with a poor shot.

At 8:30 a.m. on Monday, November 21, while waiting for the hotel shuttle for a free ride to the airport, I spoke with two young ladies from Berlin. They had been on the island for a week of touring and were flying home after a few days in Hong Kong. The bus ride took an hour to get to the domestic terminal in off and on rain showers. The temperature was perfect. At the airport, I spent about a half hour in the ANA lounge having coffee. There were only Japanese pretzels for food. However, they did have a variety of drinks.

On the ANA two-and-a-half-hour flight to Tokyo's Narita airport, the plane had extra seats, so I moved from the aisle to the window seat to take some photos upon landing. Unfortunately, it was cloudy in Tokyo. I found out that the cheapest way to the Hotel Trusty was by bus to the Hotel Sunroute Ariake then a ten-minute walk to Trusty. The four-story hotel is new and rated four stars. There is a thirty- to thirty-five-story building next door that has something to do with medical work.

I ate in the hotel restaurant that evening. When the lasagna came, I asked the waiter what it was since it was in a large soup bowl. I was thinking maybe they are giving me soup to start with. The waiter said with a sarcastic smile, "This is your lasagna." It was good.

My room is fairly small and looks out on a courtyard with fountain. There is a queen bed, desk, TV, and bathtub in the room. One thing I liked is the toilet with heated seat. The next morning, I was awoken by some shaking and then heard a loud squeaking noise from the building moving back and forth. Later, I watched the Japanese news and found out that there had been a 7.3 earthquake near Fukushima (ten miles from shore), and there was a tsunami warning for all the east coast, including Tokyo. After doing my exercises and having a buffet breakfast, I went out for a walk despite the tsunami warning. As I walked along the boardwalk, I kept looking for higher ground if needed. The walkway went over a traffic bridge, then over a canal linked to Tokyo Bay that was nearby. I walked past several high-rises, all on the right side of the walkway. One was a Shell company building. On the other side was a large Ferris wheel and shopping mall. The area is called Palette Town. The walking street ended at Tokyo Bay and continued to the left and right in opposite directions. I went to the right with a Hilton and Grand Nikko Hotel next to the bay and two adjoining shopping malls, Decks Mall and Diver City. Near the Diver City mall was a replica of the Statue of Liberty, only smaller. Further on was a nice big park and a sandy beach between the park and Tokyo Bay.

Later, I took a ferry from the Odaiba Seaside Park to Hinode Pier. There, I had a fifteen-minute walk to Hamamatsucho Japanese railroad station, thinking I might catch a train somewhere. I decided that I was in no mood to get lost on trains, so I returned to Hinode Pier. I then caught another ferry that took me to Asakusa, where there are many old shopping streets as well as a KFC, McDonald's, Burger King, and several Starbucks. After a little walk and two drumsticks and coleslaw at KFC, I returned to Asakusa Pier to take the return ride to Hinode Pier, which took about an hour. The ferry went under about a dozen bridges. As the ferry left the pier, I had a great view of Tokyo Skytree, a very tall tower with a restaurant near the top. From Hinode, I boarded another ferry back to Odaiba Seaside Park that took about twenty minutes. All the while on the ferry, I kept thinking about the tsunami warning. It would be ironic if the tsunami came and sunk the ferry since I believe I drowned in Tokyo Harbor in my last lifetime as a Japanese sailor coming into the harbor on a sailing merchant ship. I went overboard, and a shark got me. Of course, I do not know if I accidentally fell overboard or got pushed.

After leaving the ferry, I went into the first shopping mall that had all the shops usually found in big malls. There was also Starbucks, Taco Bell, and TGI Fridays on the first floor. Only one level of four tired me out, so I returned to the hotel, about a half-hour walk. The weather had been perfect with blue skies and the need for only a light jacket. Most of the leaves on the trees were yellow of various shades, and there were lots of Christmas decorations everywhere. At dinner, I had another bowl of lasagna. I was looking at the map of the area and realized Odaiba, Palette Town, and my hotel are on a big island in Tokyo Bay, Odaiba Island.

On Wednesday, I took a free bus ride around the island, then got on the elevated light rail and went from Aomi Station, near the hotel, to the end station Toyosu, then went back past Aomi to Shimbashi Station. Since it was the end station, I went back and got off at the Hilton Hotel and went to TGI Fridays at Diver City mall so I could have an early dinner. Then I had another walk around the mall going past Coca-Cola and Disney stores.

On Thursday, November 24, I woke up to rain and snow, did my stretches, and went down for breakfast. Later I packed and watched TV, which reported it was the first November snow in fifty-four years. After checking out, I took a ten-minute walk in the falling snow to the Hotel Sunbrat and caught the bus for an hour's ride to Narita.

I arrived at Narita Airport at one and had to wait until seven for my flight to Vancouver. I spent most of that time in the ANA lounge. My Air Canada flight was almost nine hours, and it arrived late morning in Vancouver. Because of the International Date Line, the plane arrived about six hours earlier on the same day I left Tokyo, November 24, Thanksgiving Day. I could have had two Thanksgiving dinners. Later, I caught the light rail (subway) for a twenty-minute ride to the nearest downtown station. From there, I took a short taxi ride to the Executive Hotel and got a nice room on the eighth floor of the nine-story hotel.

That afternoon, I went to another nearby hotel, where I got on a hop-on, hop-off old wooden trolley for a city tour. On the two-hour trolley ride, we went through Stanley Park that was big and beautiful and by many major buildings such as the conference center and city hall. Most of the buildings were new, modern high-rises. The newest building going up is the Trump Tower. The trolley driver said that housing is expensive and rents of small apartments start at $2,000/month. In the suburbs, there are lots of new homes going up, especially in the west end, where there are no industries. The east side is the poorer area of the city, where Chinatown is located. Chinatown seemed like the only area that had a few old buildings with great architecture. The driver told me that Vancouver is the most expensive city in the world per wages, following Hong Kong. The city has two million people and the most Asians in the world outside of Asia. The Chinese arrived in 1858 for the gold rush. The main industries are mining and lumbering. There were *many logs floating in the bay, ready to be loaded on ships. Later, I took a walk around the area of the hotel. On the walk, I saw many people walking their dogs. I concluded the walk with a tortellini dinner at a very exclusive Italian restaurant.*

The next morning, I took a bus ride along with about a dozen others to the Whistler Ski Area. As we left the city, the driver warned all of us that the road is very curvy in places, and we might have to wait if the road gets snowbound nearer Whistler. He smelled perfume and asked that we not spray any of it during the trip as it made him dizzy. About that time, I thought it would be funny to say "Stop the bus. I want to get off," but I restrained myself. I had a great front-row seat for viewing the road ahead and scenery on the right. The bus passed many beautiful waterfalls, and the Cypress Ski Area was just outside the city where the mountains started to have snow on their tops. The ride went up north on HY-99, and it took about two hours for the seventy-mile trip. We left at nine thirty and returned about seven o'clock. About halfway on the trip, we went through Squamish. Up to that time, the bay was on the west side of the highway with lots of ships floating about. Squamish is fairly good-sized with a Home Depot, McDonald's, A&W, 7-Eleven, Wendy's, Starbucks, and Quest University.

We arrived at Whistler in the center of a large shopping area that had four major ski lifts. There were many skiers on the beautiful slopes and in the interesting shopping areas. A Starbucks is in the central part as well as an Old Spaghetti Factory where I had a late lunch of tortellini. After lunch, I took a long walk around the area. It was getting dark as we left Whistler at four, and I could not see much on the way back except for lots of traffic going in the opposite direction. I was dropped off near the remarkable convention center on the bay that looked like a sailing ship. Near the convention center was Christchurch Cathedral. I walked back to the Executive Hotel, about a mile, on a street with lively restaurants and two theatres. The TV news that night was about Castro dying at ninety.

The next morning, I caught a United Airlines flight back to Denver. I was very happy on the three-hour trip since I got moved to first class. I also reflected on all the wonderful places I had seen and was very thankful for the healthy, safe, and interesting trip.

III

On Sunday morning, John phoned Kim and asked her if she would like to see Elitch Gardens Amusement Park in the afternoon. She agreed to meet him at his apartment at three.

After coffee and sweets at TT, John and Kim walk a couple of blocks up Little Raven Street to Elitch Gardens. They then stroll around the park and ride the Twister roller coaster, the Star Flyer, a high-flying swing ride, and several other rides. Later, on their walk back to TT, Kim thanked John for the enjoyable evening and commented on all the other scary rides that they took. As they are walking, a Tesla electric car slowly drives by towards Elitch Gardens. John notices that the driver looks like Felex, the Russian sailor who tried to kill him on several occasions. John comments to Kim that he is seeing more and more of the quiet electric cars. "I was recently on a short trip to California to see my other brother and got one at a rental place. I found it was easy to drive with lots of power."

At that moment, John spies the same car, but with its headlights off, coming behind Kim on the sidewalk at high speed. Just before the speeding car comes upon Kim, John pushes her out of the way, but he gets hit by the car and lands on the hood. He immediately grabs the windshield wipers and gets a good look at the driver. John hangs onto the wipers until the car slows down to make a right turn at the corner. When the car turns, John rolls off onto the street. As the car is speeding away, Kim runs to John and helps him up. She assists him back to his apartment. There, she bandages up a couple of bad scratches and puts ice on his bruises.

Kim says, "I think that big mean-looking man is the same monster that tried to kill me in the elevator in Atlanta. I think he is a CIA-hired assassin who killed Sidney."

John agrees and tells her about the incidents of Felex trying to kill him aboard the *Akademic Abraham* in the High Arctic and Antarctica. "I always wondered why he would want to kill me. Of course, Felex denied the encounters when questioned by the ship's captain. Perhaps he was right as the attempts could have been accidental.

"Do you mind if we visit the nearby police station to report this incident? I will ask them to put out a bulletin to keep a lookout for Felex and warn them that he is a dangerous assassin. I did see that the car had New Mexico license plates. I also have a picture of Felex that was taken in Antarctica, and the ship's captain told me his last name is Frolov."

After John makes a copy of the picture of Felex, they both prepare to go to Kim's car.

"I am sorry, Kim, that we have to walk to your car in the guest parking lot. The valet has gone home."

Kim drives several blocks to the main police station. On the way, John says, "We will have to postpone our trip to Grand Junction for a few days."

"That is okay. I will search the CIA and FBI files in the morning to see if there is any information on Felex. Maybe we can have dinner tomorrow night and exchange information on what we find."

"Okay, lets meet at the Brown Palace restaurant at six."

At the police station, John fills out a detailed report of the incident and leaves the photo of Felex with the report. The captain tells them that he will put out an all-point alert for Felex and give John a report in the morning.

As they leave the station, John asks Kim to drive to the hotel. "After I see you to your room, I will take a taxi to my apartment building."

After Kim leaves her car with the hotel valet, they go to her room. "Kim, please be careful tonight and tomorrow. I suggest you keep your door double-locked and watch out tomorrow for any sign of Felex. If you do see him following you, please seek a safe place and call the police. I am sure you have had some evasive training at the CIA Academy."

"I also have a black belt in karate and carry a revolver in my purse!"

"Wow! A gun. A black belt. Now I am not sure that I feel safer around you or scared if you get mad at me."

As John starts to leave her room, she gives him a long, loving hug and thanks him for saving her life.

Over dinner at the hotel restaurant the next night, the couple is seated at a table in the corner of the restaurant, away from other occupied tables. John starts the conversation. "I did not recognize you at first tonight. Your new look, short dyed black hair, fooled me."

"I got the new look after leaving the office early this afternoon. I am sure I will fool some of my officemates tomorrow, and I will have to get a new picture badge. I thought this would be easier than using your black wig to hide my long blond hair and wear one of your suits and a fake beard as you suggested."

After John has a good laugh, he tells Kim, "The police captain told me this morning that the car had been stolen yesterday afternoon from a couple here on vacation. The couple reported the car theft to police shortly after the car was stolen. The police found the car abandoned near Union Station about an hour after the attempt on your life. There was no information about Felex Frolov in their files. The captain told me he would keep me posted on what they find.

"After the incident with Felex in the High Arctic, I asked Tim Smith to find information on Felex in the CIA files, but at that time, I had no last name, photo, or fingerprints of him, so of course, Tim could not find anything. What did you find?"

"There was a small CIA file that listed him as a sailor, smuggler, and paid assassin. He was accused of killing a retired Canadian intelligence agent by the name of Don Cunningham, but the charges were never proven."

"Don was the same man that shared a cabin with me on the High Arctic trip. He was also with me when Felex shot at us during a hike. Felex denied the attempt on our lives and said there was a bear nearby that he tried to shoot. Apparently, he was trying to kill Don and not me."

"I think I will have to be more careful now and watch for anyone following me to and from the office. I will try and keep my new living location a secret once I find the right apartment to rent. I hope to rent one tomorrow. How about our trip to Grand Junction? Now would be a good time to leave town for several days."

"Why don't we leave on Wednesday morning at six? I can meet you in the hotel lobby."

"That is okay with me. If I find an apartment tomorrow, I will check out of the hotel before we leave town."

"I will call the manager of the uranium ore processing plant tomorrow and arrange a meeting for Thursday afternoon."

"I will tell my supervisor our plans. I told him today about the incident last night, and he also suggested precautions, including informing the FBI. By the way, thanks for dinner."

Chapter 5
The Trip to Grand Junction

I

John and Kim leave Denver about seven on Wednesday morning in Red, John's jeep, and head west on I-70. After going through the towns of Idaho Springs, Georgetown, Dillon, and over Vail Pass, they stop in Vail for a walk. "John, what a lovely drive so far. I am sure glad we agreed to drive and not fly to Grand Junction. I am also happy that I found an apartment to rent."

"I hope this trip helps you forget about the evening visit to Elitch Gardens. Maybe on our return to Denver, I can show you Breckenridge. Now we should get on the road again. Soon we will leave I-70 and take HY-24 through beautiful scenery, take some photos of an abandoned mining town near Notch Mountain, and pass through the small towns of Red Cliff and Pando, and Camp Hale, to Leadville. Along the way, you will see that old abandoned railroad tracks parallel the road. I took this exact drive earlier this year, and it was a great trip."

They have another stop, this time at Camp Hale. John comments during their short walk, "Camp Hale was constructed in 1941 to train soldiers in mountain climbing, Alpine and Nordic skiing, and cold weather survival. When it was in full operation, approximately fifteen thousand soldiers were housed here. It was decommissioned in November 1945.

"Our next stop will be in Leadville to have a short visit to the mining museum, that is, if you are interested. About twelve miles past Leadville, you will see several peaks above fourteen thousand feet. There, we will head west on HY-82, past Twin Lakes, over Independence Pass, to Aspen."

Kim comments during their stop at the summit of Independence Pass, "This portion of the ride is beautiful with great views of the leaves on Aspen trees turning yellow, orange, and red. The stop at the mining museum was also worthwhile."

"Just before we go into Aspen, we will have a short detour to the ghost town of Ashcroft. Ashcroft was a silver mining town founded in 1880. At the height of Ashcroft's prosperity, over two thousand people lived there. High transportation costs, shallow silver deposits, competition from Aspen, and ultimately in 1893, the silver market crash destroyed the viability of the town. By 1895, Ashcroft's population plummeted to one hundred. In 1912, when the U.S. Postal Service suspended mail delivery, the town's population went below fifty residents.

"Following a short walk around the ghost town, we will have a late lunch and a walk in Aspen. I would love to take you to see Maroon Bells, but now one needs a reservation to visit. I will show you a picture of it when we return to the car."

After lunch, the couple went to Glenwood Springs, where they had a walk in the downtown area and a short round trip drive through beautiful Glenwood Canyon that parallels the Colorado River. After they returned to Glenwood Springs and checked into separate rooms at the La Quinta hotel, they had dinner at the Village Inn next door to the hotel.

Over dinner, Kim asks John, "What hotel would you recommend that I make a reservation for on the night of our return to Denver? As you know, I checked out of the Brown Palace before we left Denver and placed most of my belongings in my car. The hotel agreed to my leaving my car parked at their underground valet parking level."

"I recommend TT. You are indeed welcome to stay in my guest bedroom until you can move into your own place."

"Well, thank you, John, that sounds like a wonderful idea. I can do all the cooking if you approve."

At six the next morning, they were back on I-70 going west to Grand Junction. They had a quick breakfast in Rifle and then continued the drive to Grand Junction. After their arrival, they checked into separate rooms at the Radisson Hotel next to the downtown, four-block-long pedestrian mall, lined with restaurants and various shops. Following lunch, they went to the uranium ore processing facility on the outskirts of the city to interview the plant manager.

Over dinner on the mall, they discussed what they discovered at the facility. "John, it appears like their safeguards of purified uranium, ore, and tailings from the ore processing are outstanding, and the tour of the facility with the plant manager certainly reinforced my conclusion that the plant is well guarded. He was surprised by the warning I gave him about terrorists possibly wanting some of their materials."

"I agree. Their safeguards are about what they were at Rocky Flats. All the employees must wear picture badges, and the barbed wire high fence, guards, and guard dogs should be a deterrent for anyone trying to gain unauthorized access to the facility."

Early the next morning, following a quick buffet breakfast, the couple travel southeast out of Grand Junction on Highway 50 that goes to Delta. Part way to Delta, they left Highway 50 at Whitewater and drove southwest on Highway 141 through beautiful canyons of red hills and rocks and the town of Gateway, to Vancorum. There, they headed west on Highway 90 and went through the towns of Bedrock and Paradox to the Utah border. "Here is where the highway number changes from 90 to 46. Take a look at the Colorado and Utah maps in the glovebox to see our route. At La Sal Junction, we will take the road to Canyonlands National Park and spend some time admiring the wonderful views from Looking Glass Rock and Needles Overlook."

After spending an hour in the park, they travel to Moab on Highway 191 and then spent some time driving around Arches National Park. "John, I think seeing Devils Garden and Delicate Arch was the highlights of our visit to Arches."

"I agree. Now we will get back on Highway 191, drive to I-70, and head back to Grand Junction with a short stop to see Sego Canyon Petroglyphs. Before returning to the Radisson, we will have a visit to Colorado National Monument with its beautiful sculptured red rocks."

On the way back to Grand Junction, John tells Kim, "Now the monument moves the Grand Canyon to fourth place on my list of favorite places. Yellowstone National Park is still in first place followed by Yosemite National Park."

"Well, I have not been to Yosemite, but I still have wonderful memories of my visit to the Grand Canyon and Yellowstone with Sidney years ago."

After another night at the Radisson and an early breakfast the next morning, they have a brief drive through part of Grand Mesa to see many beautiful lakes and forest-covered mountains. Then they return to I-70 and travel east.

On the drive, John tells Kim, "As I get older, I see nature in a more puzzling and questioning way such as the beauty of plants growing, the remarkable designs, colors, and smells of flowers, the variety of insects and how they know how to survive after being born, how young birds learn to fly, how animals know how to reproduce, ants working together to build an anthill and gather food, the many species of beautiful fish in the ocean, mammals in Africa, and much, much more. These things I just took for granted when I was younger. When I have time, I would like to read more about these amazing things we have on Earth and how they evolved."

"I have read a few *Wikipedia* articles on the chronology of the universe, history of the earth, human history, Charles Darwin, and even an article on the amazing ant. Did you know that there are about twenty-two thousand different species, and they evolved from wasp ancestors and are related to bees? Ants work together to support their colony and have colonized almost every landmass on Earth except Antarctica. Their success in so many different environments has been attributed to their social organization and their ability to defend themselves, modify habitats, and tap resources. They have division of labor, communication between individuals, and the ability to solve complex problems."

"One thing I do know, John, is that in the South, you do not want to get near red fire ants. Their sting is terrible. I think you know about these critters from your time at Clemson."

"To my knowledge, we are lucky in Colorado since no fire ants have been reported here."

"I believe in Darwin's work on evolution and that all species of life have descended over time from common ancestors in a process called natural selection, the basic mechanism for evolution."

"Well, I certainly believe that we evolved from apes. I see many people today that have facial features of gorillas. Felex is a good example, not that there is anything wrong with that."

"John, now you are starting to sound like Jerry Seinfeld. I think I have watched every episode of *Seinfeld*, some even twice."

"My favorite was 'The Soup Nazi.' What was yours?"

"I liked the one where Elaine said with an Australian accent, 'The dingo ate your baby.' As you know, John, a dingo is a dangerous wild dog, reddish brown in color."

"That reminds me of the conference I attended on Frazer Island, off the coast of Brisbane, Australia. There were signs everywhere stating, 'Beware of the dingos' and 'Do not feed the dingos.' On the last night of the conference, a dinner was held outside next to the hotel swimming pool. Sure enough, the dinner ended early because of a visit by several hungry dingos."

After going over Vail Pass into Frisco, they take Highway 9 to Breckenridge. Over lunch, John tells Kim a little about the old mining town. "Breckenridge was founded by prospectors mining in the nearby mountains. Skiing and tourism are now the main attractions. Margrit and I had many visits to Breckenridge with the kids. We had a time-share condo for the first week of each year, and I would always take Margrit and the kids to ski, ice-skate, and walk around town looking in the many shops. Breckenridge is where Margrit and the kids learned to ski. I got my ski lessons in a gym class at the University of Colorado, where the class would spend each Saturday at another ski area above Georgetown."

"John, this is indeed a beautiful town with the main street lined with many old buildings housing a variety of shops and restaurants."

"From here, we will continue going south on Highway 9, over Hoosier Pass, to Fairplay. There, we can have a look at the old town museum consisting of two blocks of old buildings. Finally, we will take Highway 285 to Kenosha Pass, where we can have a stop to look at the changing colors of leaves on the Aspen trees. After taking a few pictures, we can head back to Denver."

When they get back to Denver, they have a late dinner at TT. During the meal, Kim tells John about the nice apartment she has rented. "The apartment is in a new building just a few blocks from the Federal Building. The one-bedroom apartment is nice and is on the tenth floor. I plan to move in tomorrow when the movers arrive from Atlanta with my furniture."

"Congratulations on finding your own place to reside. If you need any help tomorrow, just let me know."

"Thank you, but I will rely on the movers to put the furniture where I want."

After dinner, Kim gives John her sincere thanks for a wonderful trip with a hug. "I will fix breakfast for us in the morning. Then tomorrow night, you are invited to come for dinner at my new place about six. Here is the address. Good night."

"Good night."

Before going to bed, Kim reads about another of John's trips.

On Thursday, February 4, I caught a United Airlines flight to Lisbon via La Guardia, New Jersey, arriving in Lisbon the next morning. I had about a four-hour wait for the SATA Airline plane to the Azores island of São Miguel, a two-hour flight.

The Azores are in the middle of the Atlantic Ocean, 760 nautical miles from Lisbon and 2,110 miles from New York. There are three groups of islands of volcanic origin, which some scholars believe to be the remains of the legendary Atlantis, from the archipelago. The biggest island is São Miguel, and the smallest is Corvo. The archipelago of the Azores has a climate that is temperate maritime and softened by the gentle influence of the Gulf Stream. There is little temperature variation with an average of fifty-five degrees Fahrenheit in winter and seventy-three degrees Fahrenheit in summer. Portuguese is spoken, and on some islands, it has acquired a particular accent with characteristic expressions. It is common to meet someone who speaks English or French and occasionally German.

After landing in São Miguel, I caught a taxi to the three-star Comfort Inn that is located in the center of Ponta Delgada, the largest city on the island. After checking in, I arranged a tour of the island for the next day. I then went for a walk around the city center and saw the dock area, a large walled fortress, Fort São Brás, several beautiful churches, the town hall, and the Palace of Saint Ana. There are also many other beautiful buildings that I took pictures of.

The next morning, my driver/guide, Favio, picked me up in his Mercedes van. There was already a couple in the van from Brazil. The husband is a lawyer. Then Favio picked up a Chinese language teacher and his wife. They were from Milan. He migrated from Beijing, and his wife grew up in Italy.

On the drive, Favio told us many things about the island. Because the island has several extinct volcanoes, there are many thermal springs. They utilize one large thermal spring as a source to produce half of the electric power for the island. There are numerous scenic overlooks with dazzling views. The rugged coastline is a mixture of headlands jutting out into the ocean, sheer cliffs dropping directly into the sea, sheltered coves that harbor the fragile fishing boats, and expansive bays that have been adapted as ports to provide for shipping. The mountains and tranquil valleys are covered with exuberant vegetation; breath-taking, beautiful lakes within the craters of extinct volcanoes, fumaroles, geysers, and springs of hot water; imposing peaks; and mysterious caves contrasting the carefully cultivated fields. We went to one thermal lake where there were several bathers enjoying the warm waters and visited a couple of small waterfalls.

We had a couple of stops at high points on both sides of the island to enjoy the view of the ocean and towns below, including Ponta Delgada. We also had a visit to a pineapple plantation and the second-largest city on the island, Lagoa. There, we saw a beautiful church, waterfall, and ceramic museum. About one, we stopped for a wonderful lunch. Our waitress, Ana, had a beautiful daughter, Sofia, who entertained us through the meal by showing us some of her drawings and her doll. The eight-year-old girl had the day off from school since it was Saturday. Favio recommended that on our next visit, we should fly to the second-biggest island and then take a ferry to four of the other islands. He said September is the best time to come.

After the tour, I ate at a pizzeria. The waitress was from Canton, where she taught English. She met her American husband there, and they came here and opened their own restaurant. They have three children, the eldest a sixteen-year-old boy. The pizza was great.

On Sunday, I took another walk around the city with light showers coming down now and then. I had lunch at a restaurant near the docks and explored a shopping center there.

My evening flight for Tenerife via Lisbon and Madrid was to leave at nine, so the hotel clerk let me stay until I had to go to the airport. In the afternoon, I had another walk around the downtown area. I did not see any police, and there were few people in the streets. As I was having an early dinner, a parade went by on the street between the bay and the restaurant. There was a small band and young boys and girls dressed in ball-type clothing dancing behind the band. I thought about how most shopkeepers and the hotel employees spoke English besides their native Portuguese tongue. The country of grass-covered hills and cattle in pastures reminded me of Scotland. I saw two Burger Kings and an old-style McDonald's with yellow arches during my walk.

On my way to the Canary Islands, the plane landed in Lisbon at midnight. The airport is nice and big, but it was still not pleasant to have a five-and-a-half-hour layover. My next flight was to Madrid, even a bigger and busier airport than Lisbon. At least there, I only had an hour's layover until my two-hour flight to Tenerife (one of the Canary Islands). After landing, I took about a half-hour taxi ride to the nice and big four-star Maritime Hotel. My room is on the eleventh floor, and the balcony overlooks the sea with a fantastic view of the high waves coming in and crashing on the volcanic rocks lining the shore. As the waves came in, water would shoot out of three small caves.

The next morning, after a first-class breakfast, I took a taxi to the downtown area of Puerto de la Cruz. There were many walking streets near and along the dock area with lots of shops and restaurants. At the beach, covered in black monazite sand, many surfers were having a good time on the high waves. Up in the sky were several hang gliders; a couple of them made a beach landing while I was there. Many tourists were walking around, mostly retired couples, and some speaking German as well as Spanish. The hillsides were covered in homes and apartment buildings. Dominating the island was a huge extinct volcano.

The busy island of Tenerife, with many tourists and buildings, was a sharp contrast to the Azores. I got on a small train that I thought was going to take me on a free ride around the city, but instead, it went to a large amusement park that had a zoo and water entertainment, much like Disneyland and Waterworld.

On Wednesday, February 10, my Iberia airline flight from Tenerife to Madrid was like a roller-coaster ride because of the air turbulence. The plane had a short layover for my one-hour flight to Ibiza. Ibiza is a Spanish island in the Mediterranean Sea off the eastern coast of Spain. It is the third largest of the Balearic Islands, an autonomous community of Spain. After landing in Ibiza, I took a taxi to the four-star Simbad Hotel. The hotel and my room are very nice, and the dining room is huge. Later, I took a taxi into town that I could see across the bay from my balcony. The cab driver was kind enough to drop me near the top of the fortress. It was a good thing since I had a workout walking down into the small city adjoining the harbor. Before I started my descent, I spent some time at the top overlooking the beautiful harbor and surrounding hills with lots of expensive homes. I saw only a young couple walking down, but later more and more locals came out to have their lunches at the many restaurants. The taxi driver told me that during the tourist season, the restaurants and sidewalks are packed. The weather was good as I only wore my light jacket. After a couple of hours walking about town, I had a late lunch at the Hard Rock Cafe. Later, I went back to the hotel for a hot bath. I ended the day with a delicious fillet steak for dinner in the hotel restaurant.

After a wonderful banquet breakfast at the hotel, I checked out of the hotel and went to the airport. I flew from Ibiza to Palma, Mallorca, in less than an hour. After a taxi ride and hotel check-in, I took a taxi to the massive cathedral that one can see from most parts of the city. Earlier, I had seen from the plane that the island has hills and mountains on one side and flat plains on the other side with lots of farming land and trees. It looked like a beautiful Spanish island. I saw several other churches and windmills on the taxi ride. I then took about a three-hour walk about town, got a foot massage, and ended up for an early supper at the Hard Rock Cafe. The waitress, who was from Argentina, told me that even Michael Douglas has a home on the island and probably a small yacht. Later, I went by a bay full of yachts and boats on my way back to the hotel.

The next day, I took a two-hour tour of the city on a hop-on, hop-off bus. The bus stopped at the most impressive sights such as the town hall, the cathedral, and some other churches and the castle on the hill overlooking the city. After I took a short nap at the hotel, I went out again for a walk around some new areas and then back to the cathedral. There is a statue of Lorenzo Rossello (1868–1901) that sits in front of the cathedral. Next, I went down to the Hard Rock Cafe again so I could have an early dinner of baby back ribs. Christine, the waitress from Argentina, who waited on me yesterday, asked what I had been doing all day. Jokingly, I said that I had sailed around the island in my yacht with my five-man crew. At that point, her interest in friendliness intensified. I finally told her that I was just kidding and was leaving in the morning by plane for Barcelona. After dinner, I went to the top of the museum, where there is a restaurant and excellent views of the cathedral, harbor, windmills, and castle on the hill. I waited there until sunset, which set right over the castle. It was a beautiful sight. Later, I returned to the hotel so I could have a hot bath and watch a little TV before bedtime.

After breakfast at the airport, I boarded a Swiss International Air Lines flight to Zurich at ten. The flight took two hours, whereas the continued flight to Athens took two and a half hours. Greece is an hour ahead of Switzerland. It was less than an hour's flight to Heraklion. There, I took a taxi to the very plush Galaxy Hotel and got settled in a nice room about eight. I then went for a bite to eat and, later, TV and bed. The room was unique as it had an air purifier. The balcony looked out over the city of three- to four-story white buildings—mostly apartments.

Following breakfast the next morning, I proceeded to walk around the central part of town. The weather was short-sleeve shirt unlike Zurich that was cold and rainy. I went down to Koules Castle next to the ocean and enjoyed the area. The castle was under construction for repairs. From the castle, I could see several grass-covered hills in the distance as well as a couple of high mountains covered in snow. I continued my stroll through the small city center on a nice walking street with lots of restaurants and shops.

Later, I caught a taxi and went outside the city to the Knossos Palace, a large archeological site that was once a large palace. The Minoan palace is the main site of interest at Knossos, an important city in antiquity, which was inhabited continuously from the Neolithic period until the fifth century AD. The palace was built on the Kampala Hill and had easy access to the sea and the Cretan interior. According to tradition, it was the seat of the wise king Minos. The earliest traces of inhabitation in the palace go back to the Neolithic period (7000–3000 BC). The site continued to be occupied in the pre-palatial period (3000–1900 BC), at the end of which the area was leveled for the erection of a large palace. This first palace was destroyed, probably by an earthquake, about 1700 BC. A second larger palace was built on the ruins of the old one. This was partially destroyed about 1450 BC, after which the Mycenaeans established themselves at Knossos. The palace was finally destroyed about 1350 BC by a major conflagration. The site was occupied again from the late Mycenaean period until Roman times.

On my final day on the island of Crete, I took another short walk around the city center. One funny thing I saw in the city was a guy on a motorcycle with a dog balancing himself on a seat behind the driver. Following hotel checkout, I took a taxi to the small airport.

My flight to Rhodes went through Athens. The drive from the airport to Rhodes took about twenty minutes and went through a small village. The two-lane road paralleled the ocean and had mountains on the other side of the road. As we got closer to Rhodes, there were many hotels and a variety of shops next to the road. Several large hotels dotted the mountain sides. Rhodes is a city of about one hundred thousand, and my taxi driver said the population doubles in size during the tourist season. In Rhodes, I stayed at the Best Western Plaza Hotel. The hotel was okay as was my room.

The next morning, following breakfast, I went to a bank, where I got 79 euros for $100. They charged an 8 euros fee. Next, I started my walk around the center of town and up to the castle. The small inner city sits next to a nice harbor with many docked boats and fishermen. There were few people about and certainly no tourists to speak of. The weather was great, and I did not need a jacket.

Next, I visited the old fortress that is about half a mile square. There are several gates at the fortress, and the roads inside are one lane. In most places, the road was too narrow for cars. The narrow walking streets were made of small white pebbles embedded in concrete—incredibly beautiful and unusual. It looked like at one time the whole town was within the fortress walls. John, my taxi driver, who spoke fairly good English, said it was built two thousand years ago. There were many shops and restaurants inside the fortress as well as a couple of churches.

After about a three-hour walk, I returned to the hotel for a lunch of Greek salad and later a short rest. Then I took an hour's taxi ride around the outskirts of the city. Our first stop was on an extremely high hill overlooking the city in one direction and the sea in the other direction. John said it looked like Turkey was only a few miles away. Our next stop was at the Colossus and Olympic Stadium. I had a walk by the two structures and continued down the hill where John had driven to. The stadium looked in good shape, but there was only part of the Colossus still standing. That evening, I ate again at the hotel restaurant after I had a nice massage by a lady from England. She helped my sore feet and lower back feel better. I had arranged to have John take me to the small airport the next morning.

Following breakfast, John took me to the airport. As I was waiting to board my Aegean flight to Athens, I thought about the many cats I had seen around the city; there was even one walking around in the airport.

After arriving in the big Athens airport, I spent four hours in the airline lounge so I could have some free food and drink, watch TV, and check my email before catching my flights back to the U.S.

Kim is not sleepy yet, so she reads about another of John's trips.

My trip to Indonesia started with a flight to Jakarta via Kuala Lumpur. After arrival at the nice and big Jakarta airport, I took a taxi to the Bandar International Hotel, near the airport. There is a large lake in front of the big five-star hotel that is spread out in two wings of four stories. It has a large lobby, swimming pool, spa, gym, restaurant, and business center. After getting settled in my room, I arranged a tour of the city. Unfortunately, my driver/guide did not speak much English. The smog was very thick in driving to the city, just like Bangalore and Kuala Lumpur. After arriving in Downtown Jakarta, we first cruised around the old town, with many people on the sidewalks. We passed some nice old buildings, two to four stories, and in places rubble and buildings needing restoration. There were also lots of new and nice buildings, some high-rises, near old town, including the usual American fast-food restaurants— McDonald's, Burger King, and KFC. After about an hour of driving around the city in heavy traffic, we returned to the hotel in more stop-and-go traffic. The highway had two toll booths that contributed to the slow going.

At six the next morning, I took the hotel shuttle bus to Terminal 3, domestic flights. Just like in Bangalore, there was a parking lot full of taxis waiting for passengers. I wondered how they made a living. At least it was not hot yet. Terminal 3 is separated quite a ways from the other two terminals, and it looks quite new with twenty-eight gates. It also has a Starbucks, KFC, A&W, and many other restaurants and shops of all kinds. My four-hour Garuda Indonesian flight to Ambon left Jakarta at eight and arrived at two. There was a two-hour time change between the two cities. The Ambon airport is quite small with three gates and about half-a-dozen shops. The plane's landings, taxing, and takeoffs use the same runway that is next to the ocean.

I took a taxi to the nice Swiss-Belhotel at a cost of 200,000 Indonesia Seribu rupiah (ISR). The rate at the hotel for my wonderful suite was 2,370,000 ISR, well worth it since it has a second room with TV, couch, and desk. My room looked over the city in two directions. I could see the bay and harbor surrounded by beautiful mountains on three sides. The hotel has eleven floors, a restaurant and bar, spa, and business center that I used a few times to check my email. Later, I took a walk near the hotel to exchange some money at a bank; for $100, I got 1,300,000 ISR. I felt rich! One thing I thought was strange was that I saw no Caucasians on the flight here, at the hotel, and during my walks. Nearby was a Pizza Hut and KFC. There were also three beautiful Christian churches near the hotel as well as a nice park.

The city in this area has a mix of several new high-rise buildings, ten to fifteen stories, and many one- to two-story buildings, most of which were rundown. There were narrow sidewalks, damaged in a lot of places, and heavy traffic, mainly noisy motorcycles. I had to be careful crossing the streets. Near the hotel were two schools. Several groups of grade-school kids enjoyed having their pictures taken.

That evening, I got a wonderful massage for only 200,000 ISR by a beautiful young masseuse who worked at the hotel. Before I hit the sack, I discovered a big cockroach near the door. So I opened the door and kicked him into the hallway. After that, I went around the room checking for more critters but did not find any. However, the next morning at the buffet breakfast, I saw a cockroach running around in the kettle of rice. That convinced me not to have any rice, but I did have some vegetables, fruit, and a couple of pastries with my coffee.

I had arranged a tour of the city for 11:00 a.m. My driver had a Toyota van with beautiful leather seats. I noted during the tour that most of the cars were Toyotas, and I did not see any American cars. My driver's name was Nixon, and I joked if he was as honest as our former president. Nixon spoke fairly good English and understood better than he could speak. He used his iPhone to look up some words for translation. After crossing over a long bridge and leaving the city, we passed several small villages. Each of these communities had both Christian churches and mosques. One village even had a mosque and a Christian church next to each other. There were many individual homes, mostly made from cinder blocks with tin roofs. Some were very rundown.

It took almost an hour to get to Liang Beach. When we reached the beach, I roamed around while Nixon had a bowl of soup. There were a couple of groups of teenage boys and girls running around on the pier, and some were swimming in the beautiful green waters. The beach was lovely, and the view across the bay was great. There were beautiful mountains in the area. I noted a funny thing. A white cat jumped down from a tree with a crab in his mouth and ran off to enjoy his fresh lunch. On our way back, Nixon took a different route, mainly along the seashore. There were many roadside shacks housing sellers of fruit and vegetables. I mainly saw coconuts for sale. In several places, kids were waiting for school vans. Apparently, there are two shifts at school, one in the morning and the other in the afternoon.

After the three-hour tour with Nixon, I had another walk and then a meal at KFC. I had also found a shop where I bought a baseball hat and T-shirt for my collection. I stopped at the post office to buy, write, and send three postcards to the kids. I also spent some time in front of a beautiful big white Christian church, taking a few photos. I noted that in general, the city is nice as are the people I came into contact with. A lot of folks greeted me as they walked by. It reminded me of Jayapura, Indonesia.

The next morning, following breakfast, I checked my email and caught up on my writing. A taxi picked me up at twelve thirty for my three o'clock three-hour flight to Jakarta. I had a six-hour wait at the Jakarta airport for my Japan Airlines flight to Tokyo that would arrive the next morning at seven thirty, April 8. Japan is three hours ahead of Indonesia. I spent the night at the Radisson Hotel Narita. The afternoon after my arrival at the Radisson, I took the hotel bus to the AEON shopping mall. The mall has more than fifty shops on two levels as well as some restaurants, fast-food places, including McDonald's and Starbucks. There is also a big room containing a variety of machines for kids to play on as well as several small playgrounds in the halls. The mall is very modern and first class. I also took a walk along the main street taking pictures of the nearby temple on a hill and of the many small Japanese cars. I even saw a

Chevy. On one of my visits years ago when I was staying at the Garden Hotel, I took a long walk to the park where the temple is located.

The next day, I took a Japan Airlines flight to Mumbai (Bombay) and then flew to Visakhapatnam via Bangalore and Hyderabad on Kingfisher Airlines. I was attending a nuclear conference at Gitam University for five days. The university was founded in 1983 and has about twelve thousand students. They are starting a new nuclear program and plan to have a research reactor built. The university is next to the Bay of Bengal with beautiful mountains nearby.

There were about three hundred attendees at the conference, including several old friends. The opening ceremony was held at the dental/medical school. We had to pass through the patient waiting area to get to the meeting room. Most of the talks were by Indians, and I had trouble understanding some of the speakers. My talk, titled "Destruction of Radioactive Organic Waste and Recovery of Uranium from Lignites Using Molten Salt Oxidation," was well received.

Later in the week, there was an excursion to the sights near the university. One site was Thota Konda, where there are lots of Buddhist ruins. We also went to another location called Kailash Giri, with two Hindu statues high on a mountaintop. There is a chairlift and train as well as road to the top of the mountain. On the way back to the university, we stopped by the sea, and the group I was with took a walk away from the sea and up a red sand gully surrounded by cashew trees. There are lots of red sandstone rocks and black rocks of monazite there. Then we walked down to the seashore with a beach of black monazite fines.

The meeting attendees all stayed at the four-star Hotel Green Park. Every day the maid would replace any razors, toothbrushes, toothpastes, bars of soap, or bottles of hand lotion that I used. At the university toilets, there was not any soap, so I started bringing a bar of soap each morning and leaving it by the sink. About midmorning each day, the soap would vanish without fail.

There was a Subway fast-food restaurant on campus, and I ate there a few times to avoid the Indian food at lunch.

One day there were some cultural performances that were great. At the closing session, I was the last foreign guest asked to comment on the meeting. I paid the usual congratulations and then suggested that they invite a couple of students to comment on their impression of the meeting and how they became interested in nuclear and radiochemistry. One student had a good story about a young man coming to the rescue of his girlfriend and an old man and woman. The escape vehicle could only hold the driver and another person, so the young man asked who should come along with him. The young girl suggested he stay with her and let the elders go.

There is a lot of poverty in the outlying areas near Gitam University, especially the road my taxi driver took to the airport on the last day of the conference. The driver went around the back of the main city, behind hills to avoid the terrible traffic. We went through several small villages with a highway under construction in several places, going from four lanes to two and then back to four lanes. There were lots of stray dogs roaming around as well as cows and chickens, even some goats were on the highway. The airport is not too big with only two flights that evening, one to Delhi and another to Hyderabad.

After spending most of the last night in the Bangalore airport, the plane flew out at seven o'clock for a ten-hour flight to London, arriving at one o'clock in the rain. I then caught a flight back to the U.S.

Chapter 6
Activities in the Denver Area

I

When John arrives at Kim's new residence, he pushes the outside buzzer for her apartment. Kim answers the buzzer and says, "Hello, John, I can see you on my security TV. The apartment entrance has a camera that shows who is wanting to enter the building. Please come up."

The door buzzes, opens, and John goes to the elevator for transport to Kim's apartment on the tenth floor. Kim is standing outside her door and greets John as he leaves the elevator. She welcomes him with a hug and says, "Please come in and make yourself at home. Let me take you on a quick tour of my new apartment."

"Thank you for inviting me for dinner and also for fixing breakfast this morning at TT. You are an excellent cook, and your new apartment is sure nice. The movers did an excellent job of moving you in. I also love your new look, short black hair. You are still as beautiful as ever."

"Well, thank you, Tom Cruise. Yes, I like the apartment very much, especially the security camera at the front door. The fact that it is only a couple of blocks from work is also nice. As I mentioned to you after our trip to Grand Junction, I plan to walk to the office and not drive to avoid trying to find a parking space."

Over a wonderful dinner, John warns Kim, "Please be careful and keep a lookout for Felex in case he knows where you live and work. I am fairly sure he knows where you work, so be evasive on your walks to and from work. As you told me already, you were trained for that at the CIA Academy."

"You are right. Since tall, strange-looking Felex really stands out in a crowd, he will be easy to spot. I think my new short black hair should fool him. It will be interesting to see how long it takes for my coworkers to recognize me tomorrow."

"I spoke with the Denver Police captain this morning, and he told me that they have had no luck so far in locating Felex, but his men will continue to watch for him. Your view to the west is great, and the sunset is sure beautiful tonight."

"Yes, it is, just like everything else I have seen so far in Colorado, thanks to you. Besides that, you are sure fun to with. I am a lucky gal to have you for my dear friend."

"I am the lucky one."

"I was thinking this morning about the wonderful lunches we used to have at the Plantation House in the Pendleton Old Town Square after your return to Clemson following some trips. Of course, I had to debrief you on the trips and usually got a copy of your travel diary. Your reports were valuable to the CIA, especially your trips to Iran, North Korea, and Russia."

"Thank you for financially supporting some of these trips. Of course, other trips I took were funded from my research contracts so I could attend technical meetings and give talks on my student's research. My PhD advisor commented once that his students do all the work, and he gets the fun part presenting their results at meetings. Well, I must say I really enjoy traveling, especially to countries I have never been to before. I think I told you about the Travelers Century Club that I belong to. Now I have diamond status since I have visited 320 countries and territories on the club list of 327.

"By the way, the couple that bought my home in Nederland has invited us for lunch next Saturday. I hope you can come with me. I could pick you up after breakfast so I can show you Nederland and more of Boulder. We can make a round trip, up Boulder Canyon and back through Coal Creek Canyon."

"That sounds wonderful, John. I look forward to seeing Pine Shadows."

"If you agree, on Sunday I would first like to take you through some areas similar to the Flat Irons in Boulder. Here, take a look at this Colorado map I brought so I can point out our route. We can have a drive through Red Rocks Park next to the small town of Morrison. Then drive up Bear Creek Canyon to the town of Evergreen. Evergreen Lake is where my Grandfather Czermak used to take me, my brother Bill, and cousin Don fishing. From Evergreen, we will go to HY-285, the highway we took coming back from Grand Junction. After a short ride southwest on 285, we will travel to Pine Valley Ranch Park and have a walk next to the North Fork of the South Platte River. From there, we will drive through the small towns of Pine and Buffalo Creek to Deckers. Next, we will go north to Sedalia and take Highway 85 toward Denver. On the way, we will make a short detour to see Roxborough Park that has red rock mountains similar to the Flat Irons and in Red Rocks Park. From the park, we will travel through Waterton, past Chatfield Reservoir, and over to the entrance to Deer Creek Canyon. Then we will travel through another area of beautiful red rocks and take C-470 to I-70 to Denver."

"That sounds like a wonderful trip."

After John helps Kim load the dishwasher and clean up the kitchen, he says, "Well, it is getting late, so I am sure you would like to get ready for bed." With loving hug, he thanks her for dinner and leaves for TT.

II

On Saturday morning, John picks up Kim for their ride to Nederland. After they start the hour's drive to Nederland, in a shaky voice, Kim says, "John, I had a very scary experience after leaving work yesterday. As I started my walk home, I saw Felex about a half a block behind me. I then changed my route and took a short walk over to the Sixteenth Street pedestrian mall and got on the bus through the rear entrance. Just as the bus was about to leave the stop, Felex entered the front door. Of course, the bus was crowded. At the next stop, I hurriedly left the bus with a group of passengers out the back door while bending down to hide from Felex. At that time, a large group of passengers boarded the front door of the bus that prevented Felex from exiting. After that bus pulled away from the curb, I was lucky that a bus going in the opposite direction arrived. I boarded that bus and got off at the nearest stop to my apartment and ran home. Then I called the police captain and reported Felex's location. He said he would dispatch some officers to the area to try to locate and arrest him. Later, the captain called and told me they did not have any luck in finding Felex. I plan to talk with the FBI in the Federal building on Monday to see if they can help locate the monster."

"I am so sorry. I am sure you are being more careful now. I hope you enjoy the weekend that I have planned and that it helps you to get your mind off of the brute. You are welcome to stay at my place tonight."

"Thank you, John. I told you about the papers that Sidney sent me that had information about the U.S. president asking the Ukrainian president to find something incriminating on one of the presidential candidates who had served as an American ambassador there. When I was in D.C. for Sidney's funeral, I gave the papers to a congressman I know. He told me that his committee has a formal inquiry under way into these type of activities. All I have now are Sidney's letters."

Later on the drive to Nederland, John tells Kim a little about the old mining town, Pine Shadows, and Randy and Gail. After their arrival at Pine Shadows, Randy and Gail are waiting on the porch. Following the introductions, Gail offers to show Kim the house. She tells Kim that they have a couple of college students renting the apartment above the garage. Randy offers John a walk around the property. He first asks John, "Where did you meet this beauty?"

"Back in South Carolina years ago. She was recently transferred to Denver and works for the government handling research contracts."

"Well, I would have guested that she was either a movie star or a stripper."

They both laugh.

After their visit with Randy and Gail, John takes Kim to visit the colorful tourist town of Estes Park, followed by a drive through the eastern part of Rocky Mountain National Park. Following their return to Denver, Kim thanks John for the wonderful day. "I especially liked the park and seeing so many deer and mountain sheep. I had hoped we would see a bear or a mountain lion. I was surprised by the small herd of elk in Estes Park, and the dinner we had at the restaurant of the Stanley Hotel was exceptionally good. I did see that the hotel was the same one in the movie *The Shining*."

"There have been several bear visits to Estes Park, Nederland, and even Boulder looking for food, mainly in trash cans. Maybe on our next trip we can take a drive through the entire park and return to Denver via Grand Lake, Granby, Winter Park that has a ski area, and Idaho Springs. Maybe when the ski areas open, you might want me to give you some ski lessons."

"I have always wanted to learn to ski. I do know how to water ski."

"Sometime I would also like to show you some of the places on the northern front range, such as Colorado State University in Fort Collins, and maybe even Cheyenne, Wyoming. We can also visit Garden of the Gods, Pikes Peak, and Colorado Springs. If you trust me, I can rent a small one-engine plane for half a day, and take you to see these places from the air. I do need to add some miles to my pilot's license log."

On Wednesday night, Amy hosts a birthday party for Dave. Kim and the whole family, including John's elder brother, Bill, and his wife, Kay, attend the festivities. It was a fun party in Aurora, where Dave received lots of gifts. Everyone enjoyed the food and birthday cake as well as the family reunion. The visitors all congratulate Dave and give their thanks to Amy for a wonderful time as they slowly depart. On the drive back to Denver, Kim asks John, "I thought you had two sisters?"

"They died of cancer several years ago and are now in heaven with my folks and relatives."

"I am so sorry, John. I know how hard it is to lose loved ones, and I am sure you feel the same way. I think tonight I will read about another one of your trips. I do indeed enjoy reading them, and now it will get my mind off of losing loved ones."

The main news on July 7 was about Trump's visit to Europe to attend the G-20 meeting in Hamburg. He first went to Poland for a short visit and was happily greeted by a big crowd. In Hamburg, however, were massive demonstrations with some police getting hurt. Meanwhile, Trump and Putin were meeting for the first time and discussing a variety of topics, including the Russians meddling in the election. Putin denies any involvement. They did work out a joint cease-fire for Syria, however.

My next travels would take me to Saint Pierre and Prince Edward off the coast of Nova Scotia. The main reason I wanted to visit these islands was that they are on the list of territories that the Traveler's Century Club recognizes along with all the countries in the world.

On Tuesday, July 11, I left Whit at Spot parking and flew out of DIA at 8:00 a.m. on a United Airlines three-and-a-half-hour flight to Newark. I saw New York City from my aisle seat on landing. After about a one-and-a-half-hour wait, I boarded a United Airlines flight to Montreal. I had gotten bumped up to business class, window seat. Just before takeoff, a young lady came and sat next to me. She also got moved from tourist class. She was a mechanical engineer, and of course, I had to tell her my mechanical engineer joke. She is married, works in Newark, and was going to Montreal to meet with a client. She and I had a lot to talk about during the one-and-a-half-hour flight. The descent into Montreal, a big and spread-out city, with the St. Lawrence River running through it, was extremely rough.

My troubles started after landing. I did not have a boarding pass for my flight to Saint Pierre (a territory of France), so I had to go through immigration and customs, which did not take much time. Then I took another long walk to the Air Saint-Pierre desk to get my boarding pass. The gate agent told me that I was lucky since they were going to close check-in in five minutes. Next, I had to go through security with only ten minutes till boarding time. The security lines were exceptionally long, so I went under a rope and crowded in near the front of the line to get through security quickly. Of course, I apologized to the passengers behind me, explaining that my flight would leave in ten minutes. My gate was at the other end of the airport, and it took ten minutes at a fast pace so I could make it to my flight. It was just boarding when I arrived. All the passengers were bused (similar to terminal buses at Dulles Airport) to the plane and had to go down and upstairs. The turbo prop plane was full, about forty passengers. There were a lot of young men on board who seemed to know one another. I wondered if they worked together or were in college together, like a fraternity. The flight was about three hours, and the stewardess served everyone a dinner of either a chicken sandwich or tuna salad. I had the sandwich, and it came with a small salad, bread, cheese, and cake.

Saint Pierre immigration and customs were short waits, and when I reached the arrivals hall, a good-looking tall young lady approached me and asked if I was James. She said she was the owner of the Nuits Saint-Pierre hotel and was there to give me a ride to the hotel. I knew nothing about her arrival as I expected to catch a taxi. Patricia told me a little about the city as she drove to the hotel in a nice and new Toyota sedan. Patricia has two boys, twelve and fourteen years. The ride took about fifteen minutes. The city (or town) has a population of about six thousand. After arrival, Patricia showed me to my room, number 4, on the third (top) floor. There was no check-in at all. The hotel has five rooms and was an old mansion. Patricia said it had burned down in the early 1940s and was later rebuilt. After she and her husband bought the home, they renovated it into a hotel. Then she gave me the room key that also opened and locked the front door.

After getting settled in the nice room with a dormer window, I went on a short walk around the commercial part of town. Everything was closed except for the Bar Le Rustique that had a loud band playing and was full of young folks drinking a lot. I hung out there for a while, then continued my walk around town. There was a full moon out, and its reflection in the bay was magnificent. There are several large hills nearby covered with nice colorful homes. The next morning, I was awoken at seven o'clock from a deep sleep by the ringing of bells from the church down the street. It was during a wonderful dream about being on a bike tour in the mountains.

At eight thirty, I went down to the second floor for breakfast in a small kitchen with three tables. Betsey, a nice young girl, fixed me some scrambled eggs to have with my toast, coffee, and orange juice. She arranged a tour of the island for me starting at one thirty. I told her to tell the maid that my room did not need cleaning, and Betsey said, "Good, since I am also the maid." Betsey grew up in Quebec and has been in Saint Pierre for three years. She and Patricia both speak good English. Following breakfast, I went for a long walk around the intercity. Next to the bay with several small ships in the water was a beautiful big building housing the

*post office. There, I bought three postcards with stamps. It
started to drizzle about this time, and on the way back to
the hotel, it really started to rain hard.*

*When I got back to the hotel, I was soaked. I then had
to change into some dry clothes. Next, I went down to the
small café that is part of the hotel and had lunch. The café
was very crowded with tourists off a cruise ship that had
docked in Saint Pierre for the day. Betsey was working
there. I had a nice kitsch with salad and tea. Following
lunch, I was picked up by Steve in a minivan at the nearby
tourist office. Steve is the owner of Frenchie's Tours. We
started the island tour in thick fog and light rain, so Steve
suggested I take the tour the next day. Later, I went back
to the café at the hotel for coffee and cake and saw that
Patricia was working as a waitress—she and her husband
own both the café and the hotel.*

*The rain had stopped, so I resumed my walk around
the inner city. I was taking lots of pictures of the colorful
buildings and the nearby church and bay area. In front of
the church is a statue of a seaman with a plaque stating
that the statue is a memorial for the seamen who were
lost at sea. I also had a walk out to the lighthouse on a
narrow stone walkway. In the area were four cannons.
All the streets in the inner city are one way since there is
only room for a passing car and one parked. The sidewalks
are blocked in many places with porches, doorways, and
basement entrance covers. I had to walk in the street half
the time, dodging many speeding cars. There were also lots
of tourists in the city, just like in the café. Before my arrival,
Patricia had made me a dinner reservation at the Feu de
Braise restaurant that was above the crowded bar that I
was in the night before. On the way to the restaurant, I came
upon a bachelorette party. The girls had a dressed-up goat
with them and paraded to the bar, where they invited me*

to have a drink with them. Later, I went upstairs so I could have dinner before turning in for the night.

Steve picked me up at 1:30 p.m. the next day for the island tour. I had already checked out of the hotel and had my bag with me. Steve planned to drop me off at the airport following the tour. He first picked up three more customers at the tourist information office. The parents were from Atlanta, and their good-looking daughter lives in Miami. Steve gave a lot of narrative on the two-hour tour. First, we went up to a lookout point, where we had a wonderful view of the bay and town. In one of the ports was a ferry that goes to Miquelon and Fortune ports daily. Steve explained that all of the power lines are buried and that the electric generators are powered by oil.

We then continued down the major road, which was 5 miles long, to the other side of the bay. In this area were many big new homes on acres of land. There were even a few horses grazing in the large pastures. The terrain is hilly with groves of small pine trees. The island is 16 miles square and 15 miles from Newfoundland. The sister island, Miquelon, is long and consists of two islands connected by a long sand isthmus. Its area is 130 square miles with a population of six hundred.

Steve told us a lot about himself. His mother died when he was less than a year old and was put up for adoption. He left home when he was fifteen and went to Canada to work, first as a grave digger in a local cemetery in Quebec. He then learned kickboxing and went to a Chinese island to teach the sport. He returned to Saint Pierre three years ago and started Frenchie's Tours. He hopes to get back into teaching kickboxing and hire someone to run his tour business.

On the way to our last stop on the tour, we spotted a whale. Following a short visit to a large cemetery, Steve dropped the other clients off and took me to the airport. On the one-and-a-half-hour flight to Halifax, I gained an hour *and arrived at 3:30 p.m. The Halifax airport is large. After I went through immigration and customs, I walked to the Air Canada desk for my boarding pass and then through security. I ended up in the Air Canada lounge, where I got some free food and drink. I had a three-hour wait, and after leaving the lounge, I exchanged $100 for 108 Canadian dollars.*

The plane to Charlottetown was a new experience for me. The plane was a Beechcraft 1900D operated by EVAS. The plane had only two rows of seats, both next to the windows. All but two seats were occupied by sixteen passengers. The other unusual thing was there was no cockpit door, so I could see from my seat, 4A, the pilot and copilot flying the plane.

The plane landed at 7:30 p.m., and I got a taxi. My driver was Omaiel, and he said he was from the Middle East. He resembled Robert Redford and was married with four small children. After about a twenty-minute ride to the city, he drove around the center of town. There were many old brick office buildings with stores and restaurants on the ground floor as well several old churches and a big sailing ship docked in the bay. There are two broad rivers coming into the city, the North York River and the Hillsborough Heritage River. They meet at the city and then go out to sea together. My hotel, the Rodd Charlottetown, is big and nice and had been recently renovated. My room is on the fourth floor, and on the fifth floor (top) are penthouses. The room has two beds, an old fold-out desk, a TV, and a bathtub in the bathroom. There is only one small window, but it overlooks a beautiful old church.

On Friday morning, I got up at five, did my exercises, and went for an hour walk around the inner city. I ended up at Starbucks for breakfast. Then I went back to the hotel and took a nap. The weather was short-sleeve shirt with blue skies, whereas I always needed my jacket in Saint Pierre because of the cold, wind, and the one morning rainstorm.

The inner city of Charlottetown is nice and has a shopping mall and one pedestrian-only street with several restaurants. I had both lunch and dinner at the same restaurant. In the afternoon, I had another walk on some different streets and took lots of pictures of some of the old Southern U.S.–style homes, including the deputy governor's mansion. On Saturday morning, I slept in, had breakfast at the hotel, and caught a taxi to the airport at ten o'clock. The taxi driver took a different route to the airport than the one from the airport. We passed a McDonalds, Burger King, and KFC on the way. The flight to Toronto left at noon, and I got stuck with a middle seat on a fully loaded Airbus 321. Surprisingly, the taxing and runways are the same. The flight was two hours, but I did have some nice conversations with the two elderly ladies on each side of me. One lived in Miami and the other near Toronto. The unpleasant thing about the flight was a screaming child two rows back.

On the flight to Denver from Toronto, I was on an Embraer 190 with twenty-five rows of double seats. I was sitting next to a little old lady from India who only knew a few words of English. It was a nice arrival in Denver as I had already gone through U.S. immigration and customs in Toronto.

Chapter 7
More Travels in Colorado

I

John and Kim departed Denver on Sunday before the sun started to come up. Before they reach Colorado Springs, John points out the Air Force Academy next to the mountains. John suggests they drive through the Garden of the Gods to Manitou Springs and take the cog rail train to the top of Pikes Peak. He remarks, "The drive through Manitou Springs, known for its mineral springs, is nice since the beautiful old buildings are much like the ones in Breckenridge and Central City. After we reach the summit of Pikes Peak, we can have coffee and donuts. We need to eat the special donuts there because I was told if we take them with us, they will collapse at the lower altitude. There is an annual car race and marathon up the mountain. The peak is 14,114 feet above sea level and is one of Colorado's fifty-three mountains above 14,000 feet. I think you heard at the family get-together that Eric has climbed about half of them."

After the train ride and going through Manitou Springs to Colorado Springs, Kim says, "The train ride was great, and what a view from the top of Pikes Peak. I was surprised to see that the beautiful red slanted mountains at the Garden of the Gods are just like the Flatirons in Boulder, so beautiful and breathtaking. The walk around the Cheyenne Mountain Zoo was fun. I especially liked watching the monkeys playing around."

"I liked seeing the tigers and lions the best. They are such beautiful animals. I am sure you got to see a lot of African animals when you worked in South Africa."

"Yes, my favorite places were Kruger National Park and Pilanesberg National Park."

"Now we will head southwest on Highway 115, past Fort Carson, to Canon City. I had two summer camps at Fort Carson when I was in the Army Reserve. From Canon City, we can have a stop at the Royal Gorge Bridge and Park, then have a visit to Cripple Creek for a walk around the old mining town that now has gambling, just like Blackhawk and Central City. There are many beautiful old buildings there, much like Manitou Springs. We can also try our luck at the slot machines if you wish."

On their drive back to Denver on I-25, Kim comments, "I sure enjoyed this trip. The drive through Garden of the Gods was spectacular, but I am sorry I lost $10 in Cripple Creek. It is really the first time I have ever gambled."

"Sometime we must try our luck in Central City. I have always won more money there than I lost mainly because after the first slot machine pays me some money, I go to another machine, then another. You might have noticed that I did win more money in Cripple Creek than I played."

"I'm sorry, John, but I am not interested in doing any more gambling. In fact, I have never purchased a lottery ticket."

"I usually buy a Colorado Powerball ticket once a week since some of the money goes for parks, schools, swimming pools, trails, and wildlife open spaces for every county in the state. I have always played the same numbers. Let me see if you can guess what they are. Are they my social security number, the number they assigned me in prison, the number on my Army dog tags, or my phone number?"

"I know you do not have a prison number, silly boy, so I would guess it is your phone number, not using the area code."

"You are right. I am sorry we did not have the time to visit the Black Canyon of the Gunnison National Park and the Great Sand Dunes National Park. They quite farther southwest, but I do not think they are that interesting. However, perhaps on some future trip, we can visit those two parks as well as Mesa Verde

National Park and take a ride on the steam train that runs from Durango to Silverton."

"John, I have been meaning to ask you, what is the mechanical engineer joke that I read about in your diary?"

"There is a chemist, attorney, and mechanical engineer sentenced to die on the French guillotine. A French policeman first lays the chemist under the blade and pulls the rope to release the deadly blade, but it stops near the chemist's neck, without killing him. The Frenchman tells the chemist, 'This is an act of God, so you can go free.' Then he lays the attorney down, pulls the rope, and the same thing happens, the blade stops just short of the attorney's neck. The Frenchman then says, 'This is an act of God, but since you are an attorney, you will only have to spend the rest of your life in jail.' Finally, he lays the mechanical engineer down and gets ready to pull the rope, but the engineer calls out, 'Wait, I think I see the problem.'"

Kim has a good laugh.

II

The following Saturday, John and Kim travel north to Fort Collins on I-25 to have a stroll and a meal at the Austin Restaurant. After lunch and walks around Downtown Fort Collins and Colorado State University, they head south on Highway 287 to Loveland. There, they have a visit to the downtown area of Loveland. They do the same in Longmont. On their return to Denver, they talk about what they saw. Kim comments, "Thank you for lunch, John, and for the wonderful visits to the main towns on the northern I-25 corridor. Longmont sure has some nice old buildings, and the walk around the Colorado State University campus was interesting."

"Eric attended CSU for his freshman year, then transferred to CU."

On Sunday morning, John picked up Kim, and they go west on I-70 and exit the interstate at Idaho Springs. After a short walk around the old mining town, they head south to Echo Lake. Over lunch at the Echo Lake Lodge Restaurant, Kim comments, "I sure liked our walk around part of Idaho Springs, and Echo Lake is sure beautiful with the surrounding snow-caped mountains."

"My grandpa used to take me and my brother and cousin here to fish. After we finish our nice lunch, we can have a visit to Mount Evans. It is one of the mountains in Colorado over fourteen thousand feet and is the highest peak in the Front Range of the Rocky Mountains. It also has the highest paved mountain road in North America that goes to the summit. There we will have a breathtaking view of the Denver area and the plains. After some time on top, we can drive to Golden via Evergreen and over Lookout Mountain. In Golden, we can have a short visit to the Colorado Railroad Museum."

During the walk around the old steam trains, Kim says, "These trains are sure in good shape, and the views of Denver from Mount Evans and Lookout Mountain were spectacular. I also found our short stop at Buffalo Bill's grave interesting. He was quite a guy."

"Now I suggest we return to Denver and have a visit to the Denver Art Museum. Maybe next Saturday, we can have a visit to the Denver Botanic Gardens, Museum of Nature and Science, the zoo, and the Wings Over the Rockies Air Museum. We can postpone visits to any of the places if we get tired."

"I hope you can join me for Mass at the nearby Holy Ghost Catholic Church next Sunday."

"That would be nice. Even though I am a Catholic, I have not been to church since I was married to Margrit. I do say my daily prayers before I get out of bed every morning."

Over dinner in Kim's apartment, Kim says, "We may require your assistance on another CIA assignment. It concerns a recent cyberattack by the Russians on government computers in

Washington. I will find out more this week at work if indeed we need to have you help us."

"As in the past, Kim, I am happy to help you out as much as I can. Thank you for dinner. Please keep me posted, and best wishes for a good and safe week at work."

That evening, Kim continues to read John's diaries. One entry was about a trip to the Indian Ocean Islands.

On May 2, an Uber driver picked me up at 3:00 p.m. for a ride to DIA. Jack had been driving for Uber about five years, lives in Arvada, and is retired from his job in the Jefferson County schools. After arrival at DIA and going through security, I had a thirty-minute walk before the flight. My Lufthansa flight in a Boeing 747 left Denver for Frankfurt at 5:30 p.m., an eight-and-a-half-hour flight. I had an aisle seat with no one next to me. At the window was Mike, a tall thirty-year-old fellow who was going to Barcelona, Amsterdam, and Paris to see old friends. This was his first trip to Europe. He moved to Denver about a year ago from Iowa. His job at Smash Burger requires him to go from restaurant to restaurant inspecting the food and conditions of the restaurants. On the flight, I watched three good movies: George Clooney in The Descendants, *Meryl Streep and Tom Hanks in* The Past, *and S. Ronan and L. Metcalf in* Lady Bird.

The plane landed in Frankfurt at 11:00 a.m. on May 3. Frankfurt is eight hours ahead of Denver. The Mercure Hotel shuttle bus picked me up at the airport, along with a dozen other guests. The four-star hotel is about a thirty-minute ride from the airport and is fairly nice. I will be staying here again on the last night of the trip. After check-in and a lunch of cream of broccoli soup with salmon, I took a nice walk about the area. Next door to the hotel is a big and impressive IBM building. Down the street is a supermarket, where I bought some water. The large bottle of water in the room sells for 8.5 euros, whereas this bottle, one-third the size, was less than a euro. After the walk, I checked my email, took a two-hour nap, watched a little TV, and got caught up on writing in this diary. I had dinner at the hotel.

The morning before my flight to Mauritius, I slept in, had breakfast, took a walk, and checked out at noon. While I waited for the hotel shuttle bus, I sent out the following email:

Dear Friends and Loved Ones, please help me and millions more around the world by joining the Climate Reality Project (see below). Thank you and best wishes, Jim.

The forwarded email was from the project website with a link to get materials on the project (Al Gore's).

After arriving at the airport, I got my boarding pass, went through security, and had a good walk in Terminal 1. At the boarding gate for my Condor airline flight to Mauritius, the passengers were offered upgrades to business class for 600 euros, but I decided not to spend any more money. The plane was almost full. After takeoff at four, I found out that passengers in economy class had to pay for snacks and drinks. Condor used to belong to Lufthansa, but they split and joined the Thomas Cook Group along with Cook UK and Cook Scandinavia Airlines. The Boeing B767 had two-three-two seats, and I was in the center section in an aisle seat. The middle seat was vacant. There was little legroom. The plane needed some repairs inside, especially the toilets. They served a dinner of macaroni and cheese— no other choice.

During part of the first half of the flight, I worked on a new textbook. I had bought a pair of earphones and a pass for two movies for 10 euros. The first thing I said to the stewardess, "I'm sorry, I drank a little water out of the bottle at my seat, so how much do I owe you for the water?" She laughed and said with a smile, "It's complimentary."

I first watched a great movie in German, Amelie Rennt. *The movie was about a teenage girl struggling with asthma who was taken by her divorced folks to Southern Tyrol to be cured. After some time, the teenager decides to get out of the treatment facility and meets a new friend. Together they try to reach a high mountain, where, according to an old legend, she can be healed there. The movie brought tears to my eyes as I was thinking about all the times Eric had to endure his scary asthma attacks as a boy. Mia Kasalo was great in the movie as the teenage girl. After finishing the movie, I discovered that there was a second version of the movie with English subtitles. So I watched it. During the movie, I was thinking about how Margrit did everything she could to help with Eric's asthma. She kept up on the latest treatment methods and meds. She herself was an asthmatic. I still feel sorry that I could not have done more to help them.*

Next, I started watching Argo. *It was about a member of the CIA planning and executing a rescue mission to get six embassy employees, hidden in the Canadian ambassador's home, back to the States. The home was next to the American embassy that had been under siege since the Iranians had broken in and kidnapped about fifty American staff members.*

The long flight went over Munich, Ljubljana, Tirana, Corsica, Heraklion, Luxor, Tirana, Addis Ababa, and Mogadishu, paralleling the Rea Sea on the west side. After about eight hours of the flight, we left the African continent and started flying over the Indian Ocean. At that point, we hit some terrible turbulence that threw several people in the aisle onto the laps of some of their fellow passengers. It was very scary.

The plane arrived in Mauritius at 5:30 a.m., on Saturday, May 5. The flight was ten and a half hours, and the time difference between the two cities is only two hours. My first visit to Mauritius was not nearly as brief as this one since Margrit and I relaxed on the beautiful island for three days years ago.

After a short layover, I boarded the Air Mauritius flight to Rodrigues Island. The flight was only ninety minutes, and the passengers were served a free lunch with soft drinks. The plane had two-by-two seating and was a turbo prop. I got some good pictures of the shores of both islands on takeoffs and landings. Rodrigues Island has a population of about 8,000 and Mauritius about 1.5 million. I was told that there is a small jail on Rodrigues, but there is no crime.

My driver to the Chez Corail Butte Guest House on La Ferme was waiting for me at the small Rodrigues airport. The ride took about ten minutes along a hilly road lined with farmhouses. The guesthouse has four bedrooms with baths and a large outdoor dining room. I went to the bedroom for a two-hour nap and then came down for dinner at seven. There, I met four other guests: Peggie and Luke are partners, both in their late twenties, and they live in Reunion. Luke is an electrician, and Peggie handles pension funds for the government. Visat and Jason, probably in their early forties, are both solar energy experts and live in Mauritius. Jason has a wife and two girls, seven and nine. The owner of the villa is Pearl, and her daughter, Sofia, helps around the house. The first evening, Sofia served everyone a delicious dinner. At dinner, there were numerous topics of conversation. When it came to talking about politics, they said all their relatives and friends think Trump is an idiot and do not know how he got elected. There were two geckos, not lizards, running around the dining room ceiling during dinner. I had one of the small critters in my room.

On Sunday morning, I was awoken by the lovely sound of birds at six. At seven, I went down for breakfast. After a breakfast of coffee, bread, jam, and cake, the two guys went to fish in the ocean, and the couple went diving. I took a walk near the guesthouse and met Sofia's dog, who almost bit me. The villa owners are having a room added to the house, and the concrete foundation has already been poured. In the yard is a large tree, along with beautiful flowers and vegetables. Ah-Pin picked me up at nine in his Nissan truck for a tour of the island. We first went past the airport to the François Leguat Reserve, where I went on a walk through the Grande Cavern full of beautiful stalactites with two beautiful young ladies from Hamburg, Germany, and a tall guide, Billy. His English was excellent, and he told me that they teach English in school, and everyone learns French and their native tongue as well. The two German girls, Katia and Christina, also spoke excellent English. They were in training to spend two weeks in the reserve for volunteer work. After the cavern tour, we walked through a herd of giant tortoises. There are about a thousand of them on the island.

The ride with Ah-Pin continued on the road that paralleled the beautiful green and blue waters of the Indian Ocean on one side and many hills covered with grass and beautiful flowers on the other side. There are homes scattered everywhere, most of which had vegetable gardens and goats, cows, and chickens wandering about. Additions to some of the homes were under construction. Many dogs were walking along the road in various places, and I saw only one cat. The main town, Fort Mahuia, is on the opposite side of the island from the airport. There are several other two-block-long communities with a few shops and post office. One place we stopped at was a river gorge with a tall waterfall. There is a long swinging bridge over the gorge and a bungee jump. May is the rainy season, but yesterday and today there were mostly blue skies.

Breakfast the morning of my last day in Rodrigues was interesting. I found out that Visal and Jason were there for work. They and several other workers were installing *several banks of solar collectors for the government. Visal told me a lot about solar, how units are made, how they connect with a network so no batteries are needed, why they are not damaged by hail or strong winds, and the drastic price decline since their first appearance on the market. After saying my goodbyes to Peggie, Jason, and the guys at nine and paying my bill, Ah-Pin picked me and my backpack up and took me over to the main town on the other side of the island. There, I had a nice walk around the eight blocks of the town with many shops. I mailed some postcards at the post office and exchanged $100 for 3,400 rupees, the same exchange rate at the airport. The town has some new buildings as well as old ones, and most are two to three stories. After about an hour's walk, Ah-Pin took me to the airport on the other side of the island, where I said my thanks and goodbyes to him. He invited me to stay in his guesthouse on my next visit.*

I left Rodrigues at three on an Air Mauritius flight and landed in Mauritius at five. A shuttle bus from the Holiday Inn was waiting for me, and it only took five minutes to get to the nice hotel close to the airport. After check-in and checking my email, I had a light dinner of soup and ice cream. Following dinner, I made an early night of it as I had to wake at six for my nine o'clock Air Mauritius flight to Nairobi.

There is a one-hour time difference between Kenya and Mayotte. I arrived in Nairobi at noon and left for Dzaoudzi, Mayotte, at one on a Kenya Airways flight, arriving in Dzaoudzi at 3:30 p.m. On the two-hour flight, I watched a Leonardo DiCaprio film about a CIA agent helping capture a terrorist in Iraq. The airport landing and takeoff runways ran out to the Indian Ocean on a narrow strip of land. The airport is nice and new with two departure gates on the second floor. It is located next to a much larger island that I would visit the next day. I then took a taxi to the La Rocher hotel. The ride only took at most ten minutes through two roundabouts and across a narrow strip of road to a small island with a ferry depot, my hotel, a military compound, the governor's residence, and several big homes on the hill. I found out that none of the hotel staff spoke English except for the manager, who arranged a tour of the island for me the next day.

Almost all residents I came into contact with spoke French. Most of the women wear very colorful and beautiful dresses. Some had their faces covered in white cream for some reason. Most wore scarfs over their heads as the population is mostly Muslim. The name of the small island is Dzaoudzi with the major town of Labattoir. An extinct volcano caldera is on one end. I have a nice second-story room overlooking a beautiful bay with numerous boats and yachts anchored. The ferry dock is also there where one can that take a free ferry to the main island. From my hotel room, I can see a small island and two other much smaller ones. A large hill blocks my view of the big island of Mamoudzou. There are many small towns around the big island as well as four mountains ranging in height between 1,400 and 2,000 feet. A nice asphalt road goes around the island as well as three roads that cross over from one side to the other. There are also two long coral reefs that are on opposite sides of the island. My room is nice with two windows, bathroom with tub, double bed, desk, closet, AC, and TV with ten channels in French. I understood most of the news that was mainly about the Europeans not being happy about Trump's decision to pull out of the Paris agreement with Iran concerning the elimination of their nuclear program.

Following a walk, I had dinner at the hotel restaurant. I did not like the fish, but the rice and hot vegetables were good. The next morning, I went down to a separate dining room for a very modest meal. I ate on the balcony with a great view, overlooking a small swimming pool next to the bay. There were several cats of different colors in and around the hotel grounds. Mice are probably no problem, and I only got annoyed by the many flies. At nine, my driver, Tjan, who spoke only French, picked me up for a two-and-a-half-hour tour of the small island. Tian drove through Labattoir to the Caldera. It was a hard, steep fifteen-minute walk for me as the trail was dirt with periodic big steps, where Tjan had to pull me up. The beautiful caldera is fairly large. The way back to the car was a little easier for me. Next, we went to another area, where there was a much better trail that included wooden stairs. At the end of the trail was a beautiful beach, where a couple of families were swimming. We returned to the hotel on a different road that went by the airport.

In the afternoon, I took the free ferry across the beautiful bay to the big island that took about fifteen minutes. The name of the ferry is Karihani. There were about a dozen cars and motorcycles as well as about a hundred passengers on the ferry. From the ferry, I had a walkabout the dock area for about two hours. I walked through a large tent-covered area of vendors selling everything, mostly clothes. At the other end of the tent city was a large supermarket that sold all the things one would find in any American market. There were also a variety of shops on both sides of the street as well as a restaurant, where I had a short rest and a can of water. There, I had a wonderful view of the bay and four smaller islands that I had not seen from the hotel. On the other side of the dock area was a large building that had food stalls on one end and many stalls of clothing, shoes, and other household items on the other end. I wondered how they all stayed in business since so many were selling the same things.

After my return to the small island, I had another walk about the hotel area and then bought a piece of barbecue chicken at an outdoor café. That evening, I had cooked vegetables and ice cream for dinner, watched some TV, took a bath, and made an early night of it. The next morning, I had an identical breakfast as the previous morning and then caught up on this diary. After checking out at eleven o'clock, I left my backpack at the hotel and caught the ferry to the big island again. There was some type of political rally taking place with more than a hundred people, mostly overweight ladies beautifully dressed. Some of the marchers were carrying signs. In Mauritius, a couple of guys had warned me that it was not safe here because of political unrest; they emphasized that I should take care, especially at night. After taking a few pictures and buying a tea drink, I took the ferry back to the hotel. The ferry going to the big island was packed with cars and passengers but few of both on my return.

The hotel clerk gave me my backpack, and then he had an old man accompany me back to the pier area, where he put me in a taxi. Several other passengers also got in the taxi, and after the fifteen-minute 3 euro ride, I was the only one to get off at the airport. I had a two-hour wait for the Kenya Airways flight that would leave at five, an hour late, with a stop in Maroni, Comoros. There were several other flights that were also leaving in the afternoon to Anjouan, Majunga, Paris, and Tananarive. My seat had a terrible odor, and the plane was a fully loaded old Embraer 190 with thirty-two rows of four seats for 128 passengers. Most of the passengers were in transit from Nairobi to Maroni. On the one-hour flight, I saw a double rainbow. I took lots of pictures from the window.

At one point, we flew over a large mining operation then a lava field just before landing at the Moroni airport. I continued taking pictures of the hilly palm-tree-and-house-covered area. There was a nice lady sitting next to me that spoke English. She said that she lived on another nearby island and had to get there by ferry. Just after the small number of passengers boarded, there was a beautiful sunset. Both airports had short runways for both takeoffs and landings. On the flight, we were served dinner.

The plane arrived in Nairobi at 8:00 p.m. Following immigration (visas on arrival were $50) and customs, I took a taxi to the nearby Hilton Gardens. Before bedtime, I watched a great movie starring John Travolta. In the movie, John was out to avenge many guys who were responsible for killing his wife.

I got up early the next morning to find out that my Kenya Airways flight to Luanda at eleven o'clock had been canceled and that I would have to take a flight at seven in the evening. Thus, I would miss my flight to Cabinda. I emailed my travel agent and asked her to try and get me a reservation at the Continental Hotel (the one I would be staying at on Sunday night) in Luanda. I also asked her to get me on a flight on Saturday to Cabinda as well as notifying my hotel in Cabinda that I would arrive Saturday and not Friday night.

The airline offered me an afternoon in a hotel or just a visit to the airline lounge. I chose the latter so as to avoid all the security checks again. In going to the airport this morning, my driver had the first security check about a mile from the airport, where the inspector checked out cars, another check at the entrance to the airport (body and baggage), and a third check following check-in and immigration. I watched the latest news in the airline lounge TV as I was pigging out on all the great food. The big news was about the record rains in Nigeria and the bursting of the Patel Dam, killing more than forty people. There was also news of an exchange of rockets and bombs in Syria between the Israelis and Iranians.

Surprisingly, there are lots of Chinese at the airport. They are going out on a China Eastern flight back home.

The other flights planning to leave Nairobi include the cities of Harare, Antananarivo, Entebbe, Zanzibar, Johannesburg, Dar es Salaam, Dubai, Kilimanjaro, Bujumbura, Mumbai, and Amsterdam. The Nairobi airport is nice with a spa, where I got a massage. All the people I came into contact with spoke English. An exception was a young Chinese girl who translated on her smart phone that she was scared but relieved that I was going to Luanda as well and that she was at the right gate. I also met a couple of young Indians, one of whom complained a lot about the morning flight being canceled. He thought they canceled the flight because Kenya Airways only had a handful of passengers going to Luanda. In fact, our group only numbered a dozen.

My 7:00 p.m. flight was delayed two and a half hours because of some technical issues. After we boarded, the captain came and made an announcement that there were some more mechanical problems, so we had to leave the plane for thirty minutes in a nearby bus. While we were waiting, there was a debate among our dozen whether we should reboard or wait until morning to go on a plane that was safer. Indeed, judging by the condition of the old plane, it did not seem travel worthy. The plane was a Bombardier that had two-by-two rows seating 128 people. It was one of the emptiest flights I have ever been on. During the three-and-a-half-hour flight, I watched a funny movie. Angola is two hours behind Kenya, so the plane arrived at midnight.

After going through immigration, a big guy in the arrival hall came up and started talking to me. He related to me how dangerous it is in the city and that I should take care of my valuables and watch out for guys doing a few favors and wanting tips. He also told me to watch out for money changers. The banks at the airport were closed, so I did exchange $50 with the guy since I needed some money for a taxi. I was very reluctant to have the big guy help me anymore, but he insisted to take me to the departure *hall to get my boarding pass for later that day, Saturday, May 12. At a check-in desk, I found out the terminal was for international travel and that the domestic airport was about a half mile away. So the guy insisted he walk with me to the domestic airport. Then I spotted a hotel next to a KFC. The guy went to the hotel with me, and after I checked into the shabby hotel, I gave him my thanks along with a tip. Of course, at that point, I was very relieved that I made it safely to the hotel without the big guy mugging me or worse, killing and robbing me.*

The Angola Airlines flight to Cabina left at 6:00 a.m., so I planned on getting a few hours of sleep until I had to leave for the airport at four. However, at 3:30 a.m., there was a knock on the door, and it was the same big guy wanting to escort me to the domestic terminal. I refused as I suspected this time the guy and his friend with him might take me out and rob me. So I went back to bed and slept in until 7:30 a.m. I then checked out and walked over to the international terminal, hoping to exchange more money. The bank was closed, but a shopkeeper exchanged my $50 bill for 15,000 kwanzas. Then I caught a taxi for the domestic airport, got my boarding pass for the 2:30 p.m. flight to Cabinda, took a walk, then some lunch at the nearby Fly hotel. Back at the terminal, I exchanged $100 and then went through security to the five-gate waiting area with a duty-free shop, a snack bar, and a couple of jewelry and sunglass shops.

The Angolan Airlines Boeing plane was almost fully loaded. I got put in business class, and a young boy, about five to six years, was sitting next to me, and his little sister and mother were across the aisle. Lunch was served, and I had some fun with the boy, who knew English. The flight was a little less than an hour, landing at 3:30 p.m. Surprisingly, there was an immigration check at the airport. I then took a taxi to the Spit Hotel, about a thirty-minute drive. The city is poor with lots of tin roof shacks and homes. There had just *been a downpour as mud and rocks were washed up on the road in a lot of places. The hotel is on the edge of the city next to a big, impressive old hotel that is abandoned and a soccer stadium that is also empty and not used. The four-story Spit Hotel is only a couple of years old and nice with a big outdoor swimming pool, poolside bar, big workout room, many empty conference rooms, and restaurant on the ground floor. My room is okay with a great view from the balcony of the hillside and stadium. I only saw about a dozen guests, two front desk clerks, a guard, and a clothes worker. The parking lot only had five cars parked. So far on the trip, the weather has been nice with blue skies. At the Spit Hotel, I paid $105 for the room (cash, they did not accept credit cards). I got 16,500 kwanzas for $95. In general, I found that taxi drivers were the most corrupt, and all the service personnel I came into contact with expected a big tip.*

The news on BBC that night was about the volcano in Hawaii, an ISEL knife attack in Paris, and a bombing in Jakarta. The opening of the U.S. Embassy in Jerusalem also was in the news. On Sunday, May 13, it had been raining most of the night into the morning. The Sunday breakfast only had eggs, terrible sausage, bacon, soup, and bread and butter. The coffee was too strong. I now think the hotel is four-star instead of five. After I checked out at noon, I waited until two o'clock for my driver, Mogel, to pick me up for a two-hour drive around the city in the rain. The rain stopped at three, and then lots of people started showing up in the streets. In places, there were large puddles of water where Mogel had to slowly cross. There were only a few places where small sinkholes appeared, usually next to manhole covers. In one place, a mud slide covered half of the road. The town has some new buildings, a variety of homes, some just shacks, and several Christian churches, but no mosques. There are also several abandoned buildings. A big hotel is under construction by a Chinese company, and another

Chinese construction company is building an addition to the airport. Mogel dropped me at the small airport at four o'clock.

I found out that my 9:00 p.m. Angola Airlines flight to Luanda had been canceled, so I lucked out and got on the 7:00 p.m. flight. It was interesting that at airport security in Cabina, I could bring through a half-liter bottle of water, but of course, my bag and bottle were X-rayed, and I had to walk through a metal detector. The waiting area was in one big room as the airport only had one gate. Several ladies clapped and yelled as our plane arrived.

The plane ride to Luanda was only an hour, and I was put in business class again. The plane was a rundown Boeing 737-700, just like the plane that I had flown in from Luanda. The fellow sitting next to me was from Porto, Portugal. He lives in Luanda with his Angolan-born wife. Carlos works for a gas company in Cabina, and throughout the flight, he kept releasing his own smelly gas. Apparently, he had lots of beans for dinner.

I got a taxi after landing and showed the driver the voucher for the Hotel Continental with the hotel address. The driver drove about fifteen to twenty minutes then got off the main road and drove up and down alleys in a nice neighborhood, periodically asking people walking by where the hotel was located. Finally, we got to a hotel, went inside so I could check in, and exchange $100 for kwanzas since I did not have enough to pay the driver. The clerk said they could not exchange money, and furthermore, I found out we were at the wrong hotel. The Continental was downtown, next to the large bay and ocean. It took another twenty minutes to drive to the right hotel. Again, the driver accompanied me into the hotel for his fare. I exchanged my $100 bill and checked in. The clerk saw how much the driver was charging me, 25,000 kwanzas, and started arguing with the driver. He told the driver the fare should have been *at the most 7,500 kwanzas. The argument continued and ended with a phone call to the driver's cab company. Finally, the driver accepted the 7,500. I gave the driver a tip of 1500 kwanzas on his way out the door.*

The hotel has four floors, and my room is on the third floor. My suite has two rooms, one with a TV, easy chair, and adjoining toilet. The main room has a double bed, desk/dresser, and TV. The adjoining bathroom has a big bathtub, which I enjoyed very much. The next morning, I had a walk on the promenade around a large bay. A main road paralleled the walkway and bay front. There were many skyscrapers in the area. Between the hotel and bay is a large park. After returning to the hotel, I had a nice big breakfast then returned to the room to bring this diary up to date.

At noon, I took the free hotel shuttle bus to the airport for my 2:30 p.m. Angola Airlines flight to Kinshasa. I was a little concerned about going there as it was reported on the news that there were two new cases of Ebola, and half-a-dozen people had recently died from the disease. The international departure building at the Luanda Airport is nice unlike the domestic terminal. There are many shops selling a variety of things, including refrigerator magnets and baseball hats. There are also two airline club lounges, three restaurants, and four departure gates. Lufthansa and British airline planes were parked outside, along with Angolan Airlines planes.

After an overnight in Kinshasa, I flew home via Frankfurt.

Chapter 8
Drives around the Denver Area

I

Midmorning on Saturday, Kim picked up John at his apartment building for a drive around Denver and its suburbs in her car so she can get to know the city better. John first gives her directions to get on Speer Boulevard and head southeast, past the Denver Center for the Performing Arts on the left side and CU Denver on the right side. He points out the old tramway building that housed CU Denver when he attended classes there in the mid-1960's. Now the building is a hotel. They leave Speer at Elati Street and drive south by West High School. As they drive by the school, John says, "On the left is Sunken Gardens Park, and as you can see, the school is on the right. It was organized in 1883, and the first graduation class numbered six students. In 1926, students started to use this building. My graduating class of 1960 had almost five hundred students."

"It has beautiful architecture and is big."

"This is the street I got my first and only traffic ticket. I was driving around the school with a friend in my 1932 Ford hot rod and not going to class. He wanted me to show him how fast the car could go from a dead stop to the speed limit. Of course, I did not see Officer Buster Stiger nearby and took off laying rubber in front of the school until I reached about ten miles over the speed limit. The next thing I saw in my rearview mirror was the police car's flashing light. My friend went to class, and Buster Stiger gave me a speeding and reckless driving ticket, the last one I have received to date. Buster was well-known around the school since many other students had also received tickets from him.

"Since we are fairly close to the location of my folks' first home on Pearl Street, between Ellsworth and First Avenue, let's drive by where the house used to be located. Now there is an apartment building at the old homesite."

As they are going south on Broadway, John tells Kim, "Turn left at the next street. It's First Avenue. The Mayan movie theater is on the corner where my friends and I used to watch many movies while eating popcorn and drinking cola that cost 5¢. The movie that scared me the most was *The Wizard of Oz*. Have you seen it?"

"Yes, only once, since it also scared me a lot."

"The Botanical gardens are about a mile or two from here, so let's go over there and have a short walk around the gardens and then have some lunch."

After they get to the gardens and start their walk, Kim says, "What a fascinating place. So many different kinds of plants and trees. The flowers are especially beautiful."

"It is really amazing if you believe it all started with the Big Bang. I am not talking about the popular TV show but the theory of how the universe and earth were formed and evolved as it is today. I had a little trouble understanding the *Wikipedia* articles I read about it as well as the chronology of the universe and the history of the earth. The *Wikipedia* articles about human history and Charles Darwin were much easier to comprehend.

John then gave Kim a summary of what he had read.

"John, you have a remarkable memory."

"Thank you. I used to have a photographic memory, but now I am running out of film." Kim joins John laughing. "Okay, let's head to Westwood now so I can show you the home on Irving Street, where I spent most of my school years before high school graduation and moving into an apartment with brother Bill and cousin Don. First, drive south on University Boulevard to

Alameda Avenue, then go west past Federal Boulevard to Irving Street."

When they reach Irving Street, John asks Kim to stop in a nearby parking lot. "The building across the street is where I used to work. Now the Millers Super Market building is some kind of a church. Now please drive about a mile south on Irving Street to Kentucky Avenue."

As they pass that intersection, John says, "On the left is where Irving Elementary School was located. It was demolished several years ago. Next door is Kepner Junior High. I attended both schools. A block farther south is the two-bedroom home where I grew up with my two brothers and two sisters. When I worked at Millers as a sacker, most of the time, I had to walk to work and walk home at night. Sometimes the night walk was scary since Westwood was in the bad part of town in those days, and I had to walk past a housing project where a few thugs lived. The area demographics went from mostly Latino to Asian. I think I told you about the bike rides my friends and I used to take to Central City and Tiny Town and about the fun I used to have in my home lab.

"After we have lunch, let's go to the Museum of Nature and Science and have a walk around the zoo. The Denver Zoo is not as big as the zoo in Colorado Springs but still worth a look."

On the drive to the zoo after lunch at McDonald's, Kim says, "John, I know a lot about your traveling around the world and that you have visited every country except for Somalia and Yemen. What were your best three trips?"

"My number 1 trip was my second trip to Antarctica that included going over the Antarctic Circle. The first time I took the trip, it included visits to the Falkland, South Georgia, South Orkney, and South Sandwich Islands. My second-best adventure was visiting Greenland and the High Arctic. My travels on the train from Vladivostok to Moscow was number 3. On that trip, I had a chance to visit Lake Baikal. I got my bug for traveling when I was about ten. I had an uncle who worked on a merchant ship and traveled the seven seas. During the summers when he would return to Denver, he always gave us an interesting slideshow of his travels during the previous nine months. Where have you traveled to, Kim?"

"Of course, I have not seen nearly all the places you have. I have been to most of the states and some countries in Europe and Southern Africa."

"What were the most impressive things you have seen or experienced?"

"Well, I would have to say Stonehenge, the Tower of London, the Eiffel Tower, and of course Red Square. How about you?"

"These things are not in any kind of order, but I would say seeing wild animals on African safaris, Victoria Falls, a polar bear on an ice float in the High Arctic, the Great Wall of China, Yellowstone National Park, Prague, seeing thousands of stars while camping out in Antarctica, and of course, the things on your list."

"Since we will be going to church in the morning and have more plans to see things around Denver, I need to drop you off at your apartment now since I must prepare for an important meeting on Monday. Part of the meeting will concern your assisting us."

As John is leaving Kim's car, he gives her a thank-you with a short kiss on her cheek. "John, I will pick you up in the morning at eleven thirty for the noon Mass at my church. Goodbye."

On Sunday morning, Kim picks up John, and they travel to nearby Holy Ghost Catholic church. She tells John on the short drive that she is a devout Catholic and tries to attend Mass every Sunday. John says, "As I mentioned to you, I am also a Catholic but have not been to church since the wonderful years with Margrit. I even attended a Catholic school in third grade."

John did enjoy the Mass since he was with Kim. At the end of the Mass, everyone held one another's hands in a final prayer. After everyone releases their hands, Kim hangs onto John's hand.

Then he looks at her and blows her a kiss. She returns the kiss with a smile.

Following church and lunch, they go for another ride in Kim's car. They see more of the east side of Denver and Aurora and spend the rest of the afternoon visiting the Wings Over the Rockies Air Museum.

Before returning to TT, they stop at a car wash so John can wash Kim's dirty car. John tells Kim, "I have been meaning to ask you about your Georgia license plates. I know they have not expired yet, but don't you think you should get Colorado plates soon? The Georgia plates might assist Felex in identifying your car."

"I have been waiting to get Colorado plates since I plan on trading in this car for a new Jeep. Maybe you can help me pick one out next Saturday."

"I would be happy to assist you. By the way, you are an excellent driver. After we arrive at TT, I would like to take a shower and change my clothes before we go to your apartment for dinner."

After they arrive at John's apartment building, the valet is waiting for them. He takes the car keys from Kim and tells her, "I will be going home soon, so when you leave here, you will need to pick up your car keys at the front desk."

After the couple arrives at TT, they take their coffee to the balcony to admire the view. Kim points out her car at the far end of the guest parking lot, about half a block from the building. She tells him how much she has enjoyed being with him the past several weeks. "John, I am falling in love with you."

John then takes her in his arms and gives her a long romantic kiss. He says, "I love you very much and would like to marry you someday."

"I think we need know that Felex is in police custody before we get married since you may also be in harm's way. While you are showering and getting dressed, I will read about another one of your trips. So please take your time."

On Friday, November 3, I took an Uber to DIA to take a nonstop United Airlines flight to Tokyo at one. The flight was twelve hours. My cellmate was Katherine from Birmingham. She is an artist and welds junk metal into beautiful sculptures. She was going to Okinawa to meet her boyfriend, who is a commander in the navy.

We arrived in Tokyo at 4:00 p.m. on November 4. It was 2:00 a.m. in Denver. I had watched a couple of good films on the flight. Following immigration and customs, I took a taxi to Nikko Narita Hotel. The hotel is large, ten floors, and modern. My room is small with a single bed, TV, desk, and bathroom with tub. The best thing in the room is a heated toilet seat. Following breakfast the next morning, I took the hotel shuttle bus to Terminal 1. I got there early since President Trump was to arrive and make security very tight.

My flight to Miyazaki left Narita at ten with an hour stop in Fukuoka. Between Fukuoka and Miyazaki was a beautiful mountain range covered in trees. In one place, I could see the sea. The plane landed in Miyazaki at 2:30 p.m. Surprisingly, Miyazaki is a large city and the airport nice with twenty-two gates. I took a twenty-minute taxi ride to the very luxurious Sheraton Grande Ocean Resort. The Seagaia Convention Center adjoins the hotel, and it is nice and big. The hotel is super with ten restaurants and forty-five floors. In the hotel is a large swimming pool, spa, fitness center, two shops, conference rooms, and wedding chapel. Adjacent to the hotel is a hot springs, living garden, tennis courts, and golf course that is lit up at night. Hotel-arranged activities include horseback riding, tennis, and nature walks to the ocean.

That evening, I attended the twenty-first International Solvent Extraction Conference reception. I was at the meeting to see old friends and did not attend any of the lectures the following three days. At the reception, I visited with many friends and ate lots of food. The entertainment was provided by a group of high school girls, who painted a variety of things on paper while lying on the floor.

The next morning after breakfast with some friends, I took the hotel shuttle bus past the golf club and horse-riding area to the Sumiyoshi Shrine. After spending some time at the shrine, I had a walk to the Miyazaki City Phoenix Zoo that was nearby. I spent about an hour watching various animals. Next to the zoo was an amusement park. Surprisingly, only a few people were at the zoo and park. I then returned to the hotel for lunch. In the afternoon, I went to the nearby Eda Shrine by bus then returned to the hotel very tired. The weather had been short-sleeve shirt most of the time.

In the evening, I had dinner with more of my friends in one of the hotel's restaurants. After returning to my room, I watched the main news on TV. One story was about a crazy guy killing twenty-six people and injuring another forty in Las Vegas.

After a wonderful buffet breakfast the next morning, I caught a bus to the train station. At the station, I caught another bus to the other side of the city to see Aoshima Island. On the way, the bus passed several 7-Elevens, two McDonald's, and a Starbucks. There was a KFC at the train station. The small island is connected to the mainland by a short walking bridge. In the middle of the island is a nice shrine, where I spent some time. There were two different groups of school kids there walking about the rows of unusual eroded rocks looking for crabs. One group of kids, about first grade, were wearing pink outfits and hats, and the year older group was wearing blue clothes and hats. After the island visit, I stopped at the bridge to watch a gray mother cat and her five small gray kittens. Two had short tails. I went to a nearby kiosk and purchased a small box of chicken, and after cooling it, I had some fun feeding the chicken to six appreciative cats. I had lunch at a nearby restaurant and then caught the bus for the train station. After boarding a second bus, I returned to the hotel and watched TV until bedtime.

On Wednesday, November 8, I said my goodbyes to some of my friends and took a taxi to the airport to catch my 12:30 p.m. two-hour flight to Seoul on Asiana Airlines. After taking a taxi from the Incheon International Airport to the Gimpo Airport in Seoul, I left Seoul at 5:30 p.m. on an hour's flight to Jeju City. There were many flights from Seoul to Jeju Island. I tried to get a flight at 3:00 p.m., but it was full. The plane flew down the west coast of South Korea after the sun had just set and the sky was orange. There must have been at least one hundred small and large islands off the coast; many larger ones were inhabited. As we were landing, there were dozens of lights offshore in the water. The Jeju Airport is fairly good-sized with ten gates. I had seen only a few Caucasians at both airports.

On the plane, I had read that Jeju Island had received the UNESCO-accredited titles of a Biosphere Reserve, World Nature Heritage site, and a Geopark. The New Seven Wonders Foundation selected the most beautiful natural sceneries of the world through an international vote. In November 2011, Jeju Island accomplished the great feat of being selected as one of the New Seven Wonders of Nature. The seven are as follows: Amazon rainforest (South America), Halong Bay (Vietnam), Iguazu Falls (Argentina/ Brazil), Jeju Island (Korea), Komodo Island (Indonesia), Puerto Princesa Underground River (Philippines), and Table Mountain (South Africa).

Jeju Island is located southwest of the Korean peninsula. It has been designated as Jeju Special Self-Governing Province and is the Republic of Korea's largest island. It is a volcanic island with more than 90 percent of its total area covered with basalt. Jeju is an oval-shaped island that is 44 miles from east to west and 19 miles from north to south, with Hallasan Mountain at the center. The island has a coastal ring road of 106 miles and 318 miles of coastline and has a temperate climate with temperatures that rarely drop below zero degrees. The island is home to both polar and tropical animals, 77 types of mammals, 198 species of birds, 8 kinds of reptiles and amphibians, 873 types of insects, and 74 varieties of spiders.

I took a taxi from the airport to the Best Western Hotel. The city is good-sized with many modern skyscrapers. After check-in, I took the elevator along with thirteen old ladies to my room; however, the elevator was over its weight limit since it would not move until two of the ladies got off. I had a two-block walk before dinner at McDonald's. After my Big Mac meal, I went to a nearby store that was much like a Walmart to buy some snacks. Back at the hotel, the TV news was only about Trump's visit. It did show some protestors at one of his appearances. He left South Korea today and is now in China. President Xi took the Trumps along with his wife and bodyguards through the Summer Palace.

The following morning, I checked my email and arranged a city tour. Then I went to the nearby McDonald's for breakfast. The weather was nice, blue skies and light jacket. Later, I took the Jeju City bus tour. The tour guide on the trip was nice and interesting. The young lady was full of questions for me as she had been to New York and Washington, D.C., in the past. She told me what the lights in the harbor were when I landed last night—fishing boats. On the tour, I saw many walls made from volcanic rock. She told the group that the populations of the city and island are fifty thousand and eighty thousand, respectively. Following the tour of the beautiful and interesting city, I spent some time walking around the Dongmun Traditional Market.

The next morning, I woke up with the sun, did my stretches, and had breakfast at McDonald's while waiting for the tour bus to take me to the Jeju Airport. (The bus was only $2, whereas a taxi would have been about $25). During my wait, there were a variety of cars going into the drive-through at McDonald's. Several of the cars were Chevrolet Sonics and one was electric. I had the idea that it would be great to get one of these electric cars and put a solar collector on the roof of the car. On the way to the airport, there was a parking lot with solar collectors serving as carports. There were also Pizza Huts and 7-Elevens on about every other block.

At the airport, I saw only an Aussie couple but no other Caucasians. (That would be true on Hainan Island as well.) The China Eastern Airlines plane departed Jeju City on Friday, November 10, at 2:00 p.m. There was an hour time zone change, so I gained an hour and landed at 2:25 p.m. After going through security and immigration at the big Pudong International Airport in Shanghai (the air pollution was bad), I boarded a China Eastern Airlines flight to Haikou, Hainan, at 4:20 p.m. and arrived at 7:40 p.m. The airport is large, busy, and modern. Outside the airport, a beautiful young lady approached me and showed me a picture of a room with a bed. I shook my head no. I then got a taxi for a half-hour ride to the Holiday Inn Express, Haikou West Coast. The highway to the hotel consisted of an elevated six-lane road that ran into a nice tree-lined and divided six-lane road. The hotel is okay, nothing fancy.

The next morning, I had a nice buffet breakfast of Chinese cooked vegetables, noodles, and eggs. After the late breakfast, I caught a public bus in front of the hotel and went into the downtown area, about a thirty-minute ride. The downtown area has many tall buildings, some with unique architecture. I found out that today, November 11, or 1111, is celebrated as a special shopping day, Single's Day

Shopping Spree, one of the world's largest shopping events. At the end of the bus line, I returned to the center of the shopping area and had a walk. I then took the same number bus to the other end of the city, the east end, where I bought train tickets for Sanya the next day. The area around the east train station has a lot of high-rise apartments being built. There was also a large Marriott hotel across the street.

It was raining the next day. After breakfast, I caught the train at eleven. and I had a nice, reserved window seat in first class. The train was very new and modern and was traveling about 120 miles/hour. The train first passed through beautiful palm tree-covered hills with many farms in the valleys growing a variety of fruit and vegetables with cows, water buffalo, ducks, and chickens here and there. The train first stopped in Jinyuewan, followed by another short stop in Boad, a city that hosts the annual economic conference for Asia. The train continued southward down the east coast of the island with the ocean on the left side of the tracks. The train made another stop at a large city called Lingshui, and at another called Ferghung at two fifteen. There were two more short stops at Ledong and Huangliu. The scenery was beautiful with tree-covered mountains on the right side of the tracks. At this time, a cute little girl, about three, kept going up and down the aisle, talking to everyone. The train made stops in Dongfang, Quiziwan, and Sanya. After a walk around Sanya, I caught the same type of train back to Hakou but this time on the west side of the island, leaving a landscape of mountains and returning to the flat lands of the north end. At the end of the wonderful trip, I returned to the hotel by bus. At the hotel, I checked my email, followed by dinner in the hotel's Western Restaurant.

Early on Monday morning, I went to the airport by taxi for my nine o'clock China Eastern flight to Guangzhou. On the flight to Guangzhou, there was a football (soccer) team from Oman that had won a big trophy at a tournament on Sunday. After landing at the large and modern Guangzhou airport, I had a long wait for my flight to Kota Kinabalu at two forty, arriving at six o'clock. There, I stayed at the Ming Garden Hotel, Kota Kinabalu, Sabah, North Borneo, Malaysia. The big news in the newspaper and TV was about the APEC meeting in Vietnam that was starting today. The TV showed Trump and Putin shaking hands and exchanging a few words. Putin still denies that the Russians had involvement in our presidential elections.

My room at the Ming Garden Hotel is a nice suite on the fifth floor. On Tuesday morning, I slept in, did my exercises, and took a shower. I started to go down for breakfast at ten, but I could not open the door. Then I noticed a sign on the door that stated, "Please do not use the double lock." I had to call the front desk, and the clerk got a mechanic to come up and open the door. I was thankful there had not been a fire during the night. Following breakfast, I returned to the room, caught up on this narrative, and enjoyed the nice view of some of the suburban homes, part of the downtown area, a river, and some surrounding mountains. It is a nice sunny day whereas yesterday it was raining all day.

In the early afternoon, I had a long walk at a new and big indoor shopping mall that was across a busy street from the hotel. The stores in the shopping mall had a variety of items just like any mall in the U.S. There was also a large food market and American fast-food restaurants: Burger King, Pizza Hut, KFC, and Starbucks. Later, I hired a taxi to take me around the city for two hours. My driver, Amer, spoke good English. He complained about everything—the government, taxes, traffic, Chinese tourists, etc. He has three teenage daughters and an eleven-year-old son and does not like his job, but has been doing it for nine years. We stopped at the city beach and at a nice hill with an overlook of the city for pictures. Then we went by some government buildings, the university, and a big beautiful mosque, then into the downtown shopping area.

Following my return to the shopping mall, I had dinner at a steakhouse and had a half order of baby back ribs. There was a TV playing the Canadian program Just for Laughs, *similar to the American* Candid Camera *show. I thought the best one was at a meat market showing a full-size defeathered dead chicken pooping out a raw egg when someone came by. Another one was about a guy asking a passerby to borrow his cell phone for a quick emergency call. Without the guy looking, the pranker switched the guy's cell phone with a different one in his coat pocket. The pranker's phone then began to smoke, and he threw it behind a wall, where another trickster set off a small explosive. The look on the loaner's face was total shock.*

I made an early night of it since I had a flight to Kuala Lumpur at five o'clock. The flight was two and a half hours on Malaysia Airlines. I had an hour to go through immigration and security and then had a long walk to the other side of the terminal. What made all this so bad was that the flight was half an hour late in arriving at the gate since another plane was at our gate and was delayed in departing. Finally, I got to the departure gate to find out there had been a gate change to the opposite side of the airport. Anyway, my guardian angels were looking out for me since my flight from Kuala Lumpur to Denpasar (Bali) was just boarding. It was a half an hour late in departing. The nice thing was that I was bumped up to business class and got lots of food and drink. There was a middle-aged lady in the aisle seat from India who did not say much. I watched the movie Red.

Following the three-hour flight, I had a five-hour layover in the nice Bali airport. Thus, I took a long walk from the international terminal to the domestic with a hotel dividing the two terminals. Next, I went to the airport lounge that did not have a good choice of food, but I got a chance to check my email. After some relaxing there, I had a walk about the domestic terminal and browsed the shops.

My Garuda Indonesia flight to Makassar (Celebes), Ujung Pandang Airport, left at 5:00 p.m. and was only an hour and a half, not much time for me to enjoy another business class seat. Makassar is a city on the southern side of Sulawesi Island, Indonesia. At the airport, I arranged for rides to and from the airport as well as a tour of the city, old fortress, port area, and Butterfly National Park the next day. The tour agency owner, Oscar, was my driver to the hotel as well as my guide and driver the next day. The drive to the Best Western Plus Hotel at Makassar Beach took about half an hour. The hotel upgraded my room reservation to deluxe, so I had a great corner room with views out two sides of the building overlooking half of the city and beaches.

The next morning, after a night of loud thunder, I was met by Oscar at nine thirty. It had been raining but stopped about an hour later. The ride to the national park took about an hour as it was on the other side of the airport next to a beautiful mountain range. On the way, we passed several villages and rice fields. The park has beautiful rock outcroppings, a waterfall, many butterflies, and some stray cats. It also has a butterfly museum and café. After I had about an hour walk, we returned to the city where I had two more walks, one in the pier area, where there were lots of fishing boats, and the other in an old fortress as Oscar waited in the car. During the entire trip, Oscar did not have a lot to say except that he had two teenage boys. About three, Oscar dropped me off at the hotel where I caught up on this diary, checked my email, and had a walk on the streets near the hotel. I took an early dinner since my Irian Jaya flight to Jayapura via Tembagapura leaves at five forty-five. It is a Garuda Indonesia flight that takes almost four hours. (I lose an hour because of the time zone change.)

At three thirty the next morning, Oscar's driver, an elderly, frail old man, picked me up at the hotel in his old car. He did not take the faster toll roads to the airport as Oscar had done, but the main street, leaving the city and going through the suburbs. But we did make it to the airport with plenty of time to spare. The departure hall of the airport is nice and big. I had a walk past an A&W, Dunkin' Donuts, Starbucks, and several other restaurants, as well as many shops, to my gate.

The flight to Jayapura went over many mountains covered in trees and many winding rivers, with a stop in Timika (Tembagapura). Most of the passengers got off, and less than that continued onto Jayapura. The Timika airport is small just like the town as far as I could see from the plane on landing and taking off. When I arrived at the good-sized Jayapura airport, I waited almost an hour for my reserved ride to the Aston Jayapura Hotel. There were many taxi drivers asking me if I wanted a ride. During the wait, I spoke with a big guy who was waiting for a Robert. Robert never showed, so George asked me if I wanted a ride to Jayapura. Naturally, I said yes and accompanied him to his car, where an even bigger man, George's brother, was waiting. At that point, I became worried as it reminded me of the time in Ghana where I almost took a ride with two big guys who had carried my bags out to their car while I kept asking them if they were from the Nuclear Institute where I planned to give an IAEA course. Luckily, my host showed up just as I was about to get into the potential kidnappers' car. Thus, I worried all the way to Jayapura. The ride took a little over an hour on a two-lane highway along the coast with mountains on the left side of the road. We went through a couple of small towns, and when we almost got to the city, George's brother turned quickly off on a side road that went up a narrow mountain road. George told me that it would only take ten minutes to the top, where we would *have a wonderful view of the city. I was greatly relieved when we got to the top and everyone got out and George started taking some pictures. After I took some pictures, we continued into the city as I slowly wound down from my high anxiety.*

The brothers dropped me off at the Aston hotel, which is nice with eleven floors, a spa, and a restaurant on the first floor. There are several meeting rooms on the second floor as well as a large auditorium on the top floor. Before dinner, I took a walk near the hotel. The sidewalks were damaged in a lot of places, so I had to walk around parked cars every once in a while. It was much better than in Makassar, where there were damaged and missing pieces of sidewalks everywhere. Today and yesterday, I saw no Caucasians. So far, all the folks I came into contact within the hotel and shops were very friendly and polite with smiles, but few of them spoke English.

I slept in on Saturday morning. Before going down for breakfast, I did my exercises while looking out the window at a wonderful view of the harbor, ocean, and part of the city that included a large KFC building. Following a big breakfast that included a chocolate donut, I had a walk near the hotel. I finally found a grocery store that would give me 50,000 Rupiah for $50. It was not as good as the banks, but I had tried three different banks, and they all told me that I would have to wait until Monday. One clerk in a bank told me to go to a bank. I walked down to the dock area after crossing the main street with difficulty. There were lots of traffic that never let up. At the return point of my walk was a small indoor shopping mall, where I walked around the three floors, trying to dry off a little. There had just been a short rainstorm that I got caught in.

Later, I returned to the hotel and booked a car for a ride to the airport the next morning. I spent the first part of the afternoon writing, having a late lunch at the hotel and a long walk near the hotel, but this time in some new locations. The city in this area consists of mainly small shops, with some ladies presenting their goods on blankets on the sidewalks. It is funny that one block of stores sells jewelry, another block of stores clothing, another building materials, another car parts, etc. Most of the people I went by said hi or nodded to me. One old lady came up to me and shook my hand. A large group of teenage girls waved and said hello to me from the other side of the street. I passed a karate school, and a group of girls came up to have their picture taken. Apparently, few tourists come here. I had collected toothbrushes and combs from the hotels I stayed in and put them in a bag with some money and gave the bag to an appreciative old lady. I ran into George's brother, the driver who drove the car from the airport. He came up and shook my hand and said hello, but he did not know any more English. He was in a jewelry store with his wife. All the stores and hotels were already decorated for Christmas.

That evening, I had a dinner of pizza in the hotel restaurant. Back in the room, I made an early night of it after watching CNN. The news was mainly about Mugabe, the president of Zimbabwe, who was under house arrest by the military. There was a large demonstration of people demanding his resignation. I also wrote some postcards.

After Sunday's breakfast and checking out of the hotel, I got the hotel-arranged ride to the airport. The young driver scared me with his fast and reckless driving; he even went through a red light in one of the four small towns we went through. The area airport has eight gates and is not very classy. The building has interesting architecture outside.

The plane flew out of Jayapura about noon on a Garuda Indonesian airplane. In flying out of the airport, I again saw the beautiful hills of trees and winding streams. The bay around Jayapura is spectacular. Except for the brief rainstorm, the weather had been great during my stay there. The flight to Makassar took three hours, and we were served a hot lunch.

The difficult part of the trip so far was the five-hour layover in Makassar then another five-hour layover in Bali. Of course, in Bali, I had to go through customs and immigration since I was leaving Indonesia for Japan. I paid to get into the airport lounge in Bali since I am only silver with Delta, who partners with Garuda. In the lounge, I got some food and drink and wrote postcards. Both Makassar and Bali airports were busy. In Bali, I finally saw a few Caucasians.

After my seven-hour flight to Narita airport, arriving at nine o'clock, I took a hotel shuttle bus to the Radisson Hotel Narita, where I had stayed on my last trip to Japan. Check-in was not until two, so I got the hotel shuttle that goes to Narita downtown, then to Aeon shopping mall, then back to the hotel. I got off at the shopping mall so I could have a good walk around the big indoor mall. There were lots of shoppers there as well as decorated Christmas trees.

I returned to the hotel around three, got caught up on this journal, and then went downstairs for an early dinner, followed by a little TV viewing. I was tired since I did not get much sleep on the seven-hour flight from Bali despite the fact I had seats A, B, and C in the second row of the Boeing 777 to lie down on. The computer on the plane would not let me win any games of chess, but I did fairly well on the Trivia. There were no good movies offered, but I did watch one TV show called Just Kidding, *much like* Candid Camera, *only featuring young kids pulling stunts on unsuspecting passersby.*

At breakfast the next morning, I discovered that the hotel is home to several airline crews that are taking their one- or two-day rest there. I spoke with one KLM pilot, and he thought I was a United Airlines pilot and not just a passenger. I had to check out of the hotel at eleven, so

I took the noon shuttle bus to the airport. There is a very spacious United Airlines lounge there, where I spent most of the afternoon until my five o'clock flight to Denver. I met a fellow who worked for a mining company in Thailand. The guy lived in Spokane, Washington, and had a lot to say about his work and coming to America from Germany, where he grew up. Now he is an American citizen.

I read the Japan Times *that reported on Charles Manson's death in prison. He was the cult leader who killed two people. Also, Mugabe, president of Zimbabwe, was forced to resign. I also read a book review of* Promise Me, Dad: A Year of Hope, Hardship, and Purpose *by Joe Biden. The book's story starts during the summer of 2013 when Joe Biden's eldest son, Beau, learned he had glioblastoma, a brain tumor. The vice president told no one outside family. Beau died two years later. The book relates Joe's strangeness of that period, caring for his son while fulfilling his duties as vice president. His wife and thirteen-month daughter were killed in a car accident in 1972.*

During the flight to Denver, I watched the movie Inferno, *starring Tom Hanks. It is a story of Dante's Inferno where a professor (Hanks) tries to locate a hidden supply of a virus that will eliminate all of the world's population if released. He is pursued by some bad people who want the virus released.*

The plane landed in Denver at 12:30 p.m., after ten hours of flying. I had arrived the same day I left Tokyo, Monday, November 20; the date line is remarkable. I took a super shuttle home. It had been a grand trip.

Since John had not finished getting ready to leave TT, Kim started reading about another one of his wonderful trips.

My flight left Denver at 5:00 p.m. and arrived in Los Angeles at 7:00 p.m. On the flight, I sat next to a student from Montana who will be studying conservation at James Cook University in Townsville. Most of the conversation was about my time in Australia.

After spending an hour in the United Airlines lounge at LAX, I boarded my flight to Australia that left Los Angeles at 10:30 p.m. Maria, a beautiful girl from Greece, was sitting next to me on the flight to Melbourne; she is studying aeronautical engineering at the University of Melbourne, and I told her about my planned visit to the university.

The plane arrived in Melbourne at nine thirty in the morning of the twenty-ninth. After immigration and customs, I exchanged $100 for 117 Australian dollars. I then took a bus into the city—about a thirty-minute ride. Melbourne is a big city with some unique high-rises and skyscrapers. There are also many older buildings with beautiful architecture. After reaching the city, I took a taxi ride through heavy traffic to the Park Regis Griffin Suites. I left my bag there as my taxi was waiting to take me to the University of Melbourne. The driver was from Pakistan and had been living here for three years with his wife and two daughters, seven and nine years. He told me that there are lots of jobs here, and they welcome immigrants.

After some help from a student, I found the chemical engineering building and went to Prof. George Tevin's office. We chatted a while and got caught up on our activities. We also reminisced about a short course we had conducted when I was at the University of New South Wales. George is no longer the head of the department, but one of his former students now has his old position, just like my first graduate student took my place at Clemson. George is also secretary-director of the International Nuclear Chemistry Conferences and hosted one in 1996. The conference is held every three years. This year it will be in Japan, and I hope to attend that meeting just to see old friends.

After a short visit to the white tower building, we went to the Faculty Club for lunch, then had a walk around the beautiful campus with old and new buildings. Then George took me to the Brown Tram Line by car. I caught the tram that was at no cost, and it took me around the inner city. I did this twice and then had a short walk near the old and beautiful train station.

I then did some shopping (hat, postcards, and refrigerator magnets), followed by taking the number 6 tram back to the hotel, which is in the opposite direction of the university. I had pizza that night at a nearby Pizza-Subway shop. The next morning, I returned to the university for a walk. The university has forty thousand students, and about 50 percent are Asian students. I guessed the city also has about 40 percent Asian people. There is a beautiful river, Yarra, running through the city.

Later, I took a boat cruise down the river and back that took about an hour. Next, I got on a hop-on, hop-off bus that took me around the beautiful European-style city in two hours. The main stops were Federation Square, Melbourne Aquarium, Eureka Skydeck, Crown Casino and Entertainment Complex, South Wharf, Harbor Town/ Melbourne Star, Etihad Stadium, Queen Victoria Market, Royal Melbourne Zoo, Melbourne Museum, Chinatown, Cathedral Place, Fitzroy Gardens, and the sports precinct.

Saturday was much cooler than yesterday. I took another bus ride today, but this one went in the opposite direction of the city, past my hotel, to St. Kilda beach. The main stops were Federation Square, Shrine of Remembrance, South Melbourne, Pullman Hotel, the Esplanade St. Kilda, Luna Park/Palais Theater, St. Kilda Marina, St. Kilda State Park, South Melbourne Beach, Station Pier/Port Melbourne, Bay Street, Crown Casino and Entertainment Complex, and Arts Center Melbourne.

On the bus tour, I had the front seat, and a nice lady from Hamburg sat across the aisle. She owns a realty business in Germany and has traveled a lot. Her son is a mechanical engineer, and her daughter is in medical school. Of course, I told her my mechanical engineer joke to tell her son. St. Kilda is a nice resort town, and I walked part way back, about ten blocks past many pubs and restaurants, then caught a tram back to the hotel. Across from the hotel is a college for the deaf, and next to it is another college that had a big outdoor restaurant that was full of noisy college students drinking and eating. I joined the fun and had dinner. Then I had a walk around the college campus and fought off some pesky flies that kept trying to get in my eyes.

I checked out of the hotel Sunday morning after I did my exercises and had breakfast in the room. I usually leave a tip in the room for the maid, but this time I hid five $1 coins around the room in various places where the maid would easily find them, such as under the dirty towels on the bathroom floor and under the waste basket. I took a tram into the city and had a short visit at St. Paul's Church that is diagonally across from the Flinders Street tram station. Across from the church is a nice visitor's center. I went back to the hotel in the afternoon to collect my backpack and to catch the airport bus, arriving there about four.

My flight to Auckland left at eight and arrived there at midnight. I had a seven-hour wait for my Air New Zealand flight to Queenstown and tried without success to sleep. About five o'clock, I took a twenty-minute walk from the international terminal to the domestic terminal, where, following a security check, I went to the nice New Zealand Air lounge. There, I had a nice breakfast and checked my email. At seven, my flight to Queenstown left Auckland. The flight was only two hours. A couple from San Diego was sitting next to me, and they described their experiences on a big cruise ship that lost engine power off the coast of

Brisbane. They were stranded for two days and had to fly into Auckland instead of going by sea. The cruise company refunded their fare for the trip.

On the descent into Queenstown, the plane ran into some bad turbulence that made our stewardess quickly sit on the floor. Right before landing, I could see some beautiful snowcapped mountains in one direction and green hills in the other direction. Lake Wakatipu is near the small airport and is New Zealand's longest lake. After landing, I took a taxi to the Doubletree Hotel that is next to the Hilton on the opposite side of the lake from Queenstown. The only way into the city from the hotel, other than a long walk or swimming, is either by taxi, hotel shuttle bus (free), or water taxi ($10). There is a golf course nearby. I read in the newspaper that Oprah Winfrey and Reese Witherspoon were in town to shoot a movie. The other major news were fires in New South Wales near Dondingalong and a 6.5 earthquake in Indonesia, where I had been last November.

Following check-in, I took the water taxi, a half-hour ride across Lake Wakatipu, to Queenstown, and then the gondola up to the top of a mountain that overlooks the city and a beautiful mountain range. There was a dusting of snow on the tops of the mountains that had occurred a few days earlier and what the taxi driver said was unusual for this to happen in the summer. Near the exit of the gondola was a gift shop, restaurant, entrances to sky diving, bungee jumping, and a chairlift to the very top where one could ride a type of go-cart called luge back to the gondola area. In the area, one could take helicopter and small plane flights over Milford Sound, widely acknowledged as one of the world's most scenic areas. There, one can see beautiful mountain lakes, fjords, and the lush rainforests of Fjordland National Park. There is also jet boating, kayaking, and rafting on Lake Wakatipu and on the river that exits the lake as well as mountain biking and hiking on numerous trails in the area.

Another thing that can be done in this touristy town, which goes from a population of thirty thousand to almost two hundred thousand during the tourist season, is taking a ride on the TSS Earnslaw, *a steam ship built in 1912, which goes across Wakatipu. It was named after Mount Earnslaw, the highest peak in the region. There is also Kiwi Birdlife Park, mini golf, waterskiing, and horseback riding. In the winter, one could snow ski at the nearby Cardrona resort with three basins of skiing.*

I left Queenstown by bus on Thursday, February 16, at 8:00 a.m. and arrived in Dunedin at noon. On the trip, the bus first had to go over the river exiting Lake Wakatipu on a one-lane bridge. Traffic was controlled by workmen (usually there is a stoplight) who were constructing a second bridge so that there would be two lanes for cars. The same thing was required on the taxi ride from the airport as well as the two days I took the hotel shuttle bus into town. On the bus to Dunedin, the highway went through numerous canyons surrounded by snow-capped mountains and later grass-covered hills with many sheep grazing. The major cities we went through were Cromwell, Alexandra, Lawrence, and Milton. The Milton HY-8 that the bus had traveled on ran into HY-1 that went to Dunedin one way and to Invercargill the other. There were many farms, orchards, and vineyards during the last hour of the trip into Dunedin. In Dunedin, I had lunch at a café near the bus station. I heard that the Cadbury chocolate factory was closing, the only Cadbury manufacturer in New Zealand. Now the Cadbury bars will come from Australia.

On the ride to Te Anau, I got acquainted with two young ladies from Germany. They had been traveling around New Zealand for three months and spent about a month in Wellington working. One gal worked as a waitress and the other for a charity organization. The girls plan to return to college in a month following their New Zealand adventures.

They got off the bus in Gore, where they boarded a different bus to Invercargill. It was funny that the small town we passed through before we got to Gore was Clinton. In Gore, there is a nice golf course and a sign saying Gore is the capital of country music. About 3:30 p.m., the bus had a thirty-minute stop at Pegs Dale, where there was only a café and gift shop. (I bought a shirt.) During the last part of the trip, I continued to see rolling green grass hills covered with sheep and cattle and even a couple of ranches with fenced-in deer herds. There were also lots of farms growing grapes, wheat, and vegetables.

About 6:00 p.m., the highway crossed HY-6 that went north to Queenstown, and south to Invercargill. The bus arrived in Te Anau about an hour later. I checked into the Village Inn Hotel, a three-star that was nice. My room had two double beds and was quite spacious. The small town is only about four-by-four blocks with a large park, Subway, and several other fine restaurants and shops. Te Anau has a population of about four thousand, and annually it receives about ten thousand tourists. After a walk about the main part of town, I had dinner at an Italian restaurant. One of the nearby street signs in Te Anau was named "Wrong Way." I later went to the dock area of Lake Te Anau that was on the north edge of the town center. The waters of Lake Te Anan come from glaciers in the surrounding mountains and supplies most of the fresh water for the area.

The next morning, I caught a tour bus and traveled along the spectacular alpine route to Milford Sound, considered one of the most beautiful drives in the world. Milford Sound is New Zealand's only fjord accessible by road. The highway was good, and the trip of about one hundred miles took two hours. Just before we got to the one-lane Homer Tunnel, we passed Divide, where the range separates west from east New Zealand. The tunnel is about a half a mile long and was dug by workmen using only picks and shovels during the

1930s. The road has several areas where it is often closed in the winter because of avalanches. During most of the winter, it is cleared by snowplows. Te Anau has no snowplows since it only gets one or two minor snowstorms each winter. I was told that it does get very cold and windy though. On the drive, we passed through Fjordland National Park.

The bus was nice as it had glass roofs above every seat. There were several stops along the Milford Road with time for short walks and photo opportunities. The coach driver provided detailed commentaries throughout the trip. On reaching Milford Sound, I boarded the Mariner ship that had three levels and was about forty feet long with restaurant. The two-hour cruise provided fantastic views of many thin and tall waterfalls coming off the snow-capped rugged peaks. Our tour group was lucky as we saw some seals, dolphins, and penguins. The weather was blue skies and warm with only the need for a light jacket.

Following the cruise, I returned to Te Anau. That evening, I had another walk about town and ate at a Western restaurant, where I had a small order of terrible baby back ribs. The next morning, Saturday, February 18, I got caught up on my diary writing after sleeping in and having a small breakfast in the room. In the afternoon, I had another walk about town in my new short-sleeve shirt—no jacked needed.

On Sunday morning, I caught the tour bus at eight to Invercargill via a bus change in Gore. At the bus stop, I spoke with a young lady from France. She had been traveling New Zealand for a year and working at several places during the year doing a variety of jobs. The scenery on the way to Invercargill was through a wide valley with beautiful green hills on both sides. There were many farms growing wheat, hay, and vegetables as well as ranches with sheep, cattle, and some with deer. The bus arrived at Invercargill at eleven o'clock, and I checked into the Kelvin Hotel after a short taxi ride from the bus stop at the museum. Invercargill is New

Zealand's most southern city with a population of fifty-two thousand people. The building housing the museum and art gallery is the largest pyramid structure in the southern hemisphere. I had a walk about the middle of town, about six square blocks, and then went to the nearby Biker Café for a big, late breakfast. Later, I returned to the hotel, where I booked a trip to Stewart Island in the morning.

A bus picked me up at eight o'clock the next morning and went to Bluff, where I took a one-hour catamaran ride across Foveaux Strait at nine thirty to Stewart Island. The island does not get any snow, and the average temperature is about forty degrees in winter and seventy-five degrees in summer, but it does get lots of rain. The island has forested hills descending to a coastline of rocky outcrops and golden sandy beaches and is surrounded by 170 smaller islands. It is a natural refuge for marine and bird life. I paid a visit to Rakiura National Park, New Zealand's southernmost national park; 85 percent of the park belongs to the main island. Rakiura is one of the Maori names given to the island, which receives glowing sunrises, sunsets, and the aurora australis or "southern lights." I was told that there are more kiwis and white-tailed deer on the island than the 386 humans; 30 percent of kiwis in New Zealand are on Stewart Island. The island inhabitants are extremely healthy as their main diet is venison, vegetables, and fish. The main income for the island comes from tourism and fishing.

I also spent some time in the village of Maori, where I had lunch and saw a couple of churches, a fire station, a museum, a hotel, several small hospitals, an elementary school (the older students attend a high school in Invercargill), a New Zealand visitor center, a gas station, an airport (they have three flights each day to Invercargill), and some of the homes for the 386 inhabitants. The school has 29 students, 2 teachers, and a principal. I took a one-and-a-half-hour bus tour of the town and the outskirts of Oban. The tour driver told me and the other three passengers a lot about the town and island. He said they have a rugby court that is used once a year, there is no crime, and the sheriff has a one-cell jail in his office. He uses it to store his home brew. One time he did make an arrest of a guy who had drank too much at the hotel bar and was causing trouble. He put the drunk in the cell and forgot he had his home brew in there. The next morning, the drunk was even drunker. The town also has a six-hole golf course, so players must play the six holes three times.

I returned to Buff at 5:00 p.m. The catamaran ride from Stewart Island was rough despite the pleasant temperature. Bluff is the oldest European town in New Zealand, having been settled continuously since 1824. In Bluff, the bus was waiting to take me back to Invercargill. The ride took about thirty minutes. A funny sign in Bluff stated, "Where the highway begins." Bluff has a population of about four hundred.

Back at the Hotel Kevin, which has a casino, I put $5 in a slot machine, and I won $35. The next morning, Tuesday, February 22, I had another walk and spent some time admiring the magnificent Church of Mary. Then I took a long walk down to Queen Park. Next to the park was Invercargill's 120-foot-high water tower that was built in 1889 using three hundred thousand bricks. The tower is part of the city's main water supply system. Because of concerns about earthquake safety, the tower is no longer open to the public. The park is very large (about ten square blocks) and has cricket grounds, golf course, Japanese garden, small zoo, playground, museum, and art gallery. In the zoo, there was a tuatara, about a foot long, that looks like a lizard but belongs to another reptile family. The park has lots of flowers, a rose garden, and many varieties of trees all surrounded by grass. The park is so big that I got lost and had to ask for directions twice. Near the park is a

McDonald's, where I had lunch. Then I had an eight-block walk back to the hotel. In the afternoon, I took a long hot bath in a big tub, caught up on this diary, and edited my photos. That evening, I went for another stroll with few people about. It looked like the pubs and restaurants had lots of patrons. I had dinner at the hotel and went to bed early. The hotel had an interesting notice on my door about what to do in case of an earthquake—"Pray."

On Thursday, February 22, I took a taxi to the park and caught the bus to Dunedin with a half-hour break at Pegs Dale, just like the trip from Dunedin to Te Anau via Gore, a few days earlier. After I arrived at the Dunedin bus station, I took a ten-minute walk to the train station. There, I booked a trip for the next morning on the Seasider Train. Then I took a taxi to the Best Western Hotel on Bayview next to Anderson Bay Road.

Later, I caught the number 11 bus back into town instead of the thirty-minute walk. There, I had a walk and an early dinner. I sat at an outdoor restaurant but still smelled marijuana smoke in the air. It felt like my first visit to Dunedin last November was only a couple of weeks ago. Now Dunedin is my favorite New Zealand city with Queenstown in second place.

The main story on the news was the opening of a memorial wall with the names of the 185 people killed in the Christchurch earthquake six years ago. Bruce Springsteen was there to give a memorial concert. There were visitors from many other countries at the memorial. I recalled a smaller earthquake Christchurch had a few days after my visit there last November. The other news was the forest fire near Christchurch that had raged for several days.

Historic Dunedin has an abundance of Victorian and Edwardian architecture that I loved and which I took many pictures of, just like the trip here last November. The city stretches around a long and beautiful harbor sheltered by the stunning Otago Peninsula, home to a colony of one of the world's rarest penguins, the yellow-eyed penguin. It also boasts the only mainland breeding colony of the Royal Albatross, and its rugged coastline is frequented by rare New Zealand Hooker Sea Lions. Maori have occupied the south of the South Island for approximately one thousand years. Kai Tahu Whanui are the indigenous people of the southern islands of New Zealand. In the late 1500s, Kati Mamoe arrived from the Wellington area. Soon after, they were followed across Cook Strait/Te Moana a Raukawa by two powerful Ngai Tahu hapu/clan groupings, arriving over the space of two generations. By the mid-eighteenth century, the three had fused into one iwi. In 1800, there were about twenty thousand people calling themselves Kai Tahu or Nagai Tahu; however, there were still groupings of people, particularly in the south, who maintained a strong Kati Mamoe identity. Today Kai Tahu people remain a strong tribe in the south, their influence being visible throughout the Southern Scenic Route.

The first European visitors to the south were sealers. Whaling was the next industry, and Riverton was established as a base by John Howell in 1836. As European explorers ventured inland, they paved the way for pioneering farmers. In 1861, gold was discovered. Several gold rushes ensued with thousands of prospectors arriving, some from Australia and China, to exploit gold in the Shotover and Arrow rivers (among other places). Dunedin also benefited from the gold rush days, briefly becoming New Zealand's largest town. Sawmills have also been an important part of the south's history. From axes and bullocks, the industry developed sophisticated steam-powered haulers, locomotives, and mills. The Owaka River was also a site of immense activity— in 1872, more timber left the Owaka River than any other South Island port. In the 1920s, the mill at Port Craig was the largest in the country. Construction of a railway line from Balclutha began in 1879, reaching Owaka in 1896, and its final railhead at Tahakopa in 1915. In its wake followed sawmills, schools, and farms. As the accessible forests were milled and burned, pioneer farmers turned the land to agricultural use. Hydroelectric development of the Waiau Valley began in 1925, raising the level of Lake Monowai for power generation. In 1971, the Manapouri hydro station was completed, diverting water from Lakes Te Anau and Manapouri to Doubtful Sound/Patea and supplying power to the Tiwai Point aluminum smelter near Bluff.

In Maori legend, the Dunedin's harbor was formed by Matamata, the largest of all taniwha (water monster), which slept there leaving a depression that filled with sea water. Capt. James Cook marked Otago Peninsula on his charts, naming Cape Saunders in 1770. There are records of sailing ships entering the harbor as early as 1803, with the first European migrants arriving at Port Chalmers in 1848 before moving to Otepoti to build their new city. Otago Harbor has three berths: Dunedin, Port Chalmers, and Ravensbourne. The harbor is naturally shallow, and the artificial Victoria Channel is constantly dredged to provide deep water access to Dunedin's wharves. Port Chalmers is where Dunedin and Otago began with the arrival of the first European settlers' ships in 1848. Port Chalmers was made famous by the visit in 1910 of polar explorer Robert Falcon Scott on his ill-fated journey to the South Pole. Today Port Chalmers is one of New Zealand's busiest ports with a container terminal and logging facility. It is also the destination of many visiting international cruise ships.

Dunedin sits in a large valley surrounded by tree- and grass-covered hills, a beautiful area. The major industry in town is a Speights Brewery and Cadbury facility, the only one in the country, but as stated above, it is shutting down because of low profits. Dunedin has a population of about one hundred thousand with twenty thousand university students. The main street, Princes, has a name change to George Street at the center of the city. Tonight it is alive and full of people, mainly with tourists and returning students, some walking around drinking beer and wine from bottles. This was a great contrast from Invercargill as I saw very few people on the sidewalks there after the shops closed at six. Most of the shops in Dunedin stay open in the evening. The restaurants had sidewalk tables with many customers having dinner as well as young folks filling up Starbucks, McDonald's, Burger King, and KFC. I was told that classes start next week, and many of the students' families are in town. To vouch for this, there were "no vacancy" signs on all the hotels/motels that I saw. As my motel is quite a ways from Otago University, it was not surprising that there were vacancies there. My room is genuinely nice by the way. Around my motel area are the same fast-food restaurants as in the city as well as a few new car dealers, two large supermarkets, and a big building materials store like Home Depot in the U.S.

I boarded the Seasider train at ten the next morning for a ninety-minute ride north along the ocean. The Seasider is a unique train journey from Dunedin to either Waitati, Moeraki Boulders, or Oamuru and return, offering some of the most spectacular coastal scenery in New Zealand. The line on which I traveled is part of the main trunk line of the South Island. The Dunedin-Palmerston section of line was completed in 1879, but it was not until 1945 that the entire line was completed from Picton to Bluff.

On the ride, the train first went by Otago Harbor, where there was a merchant and large cruise ship anchored. The ride continued with water on the right side and rolling hills of trees and shrubs on the other. The train went through Port Chalmers and Purakaunui to Waitati then returned to Dunedin after the conductor reversed the direction of the seats. There were only two cars on the train. The two rows of seats in front of me had a table between them. Four elderly people were sitting together there, and at Waitati, I found out that they were all from a small city near São Paulo, Brazil. One lady discussed my visit to Brazil's northeast and what I do for work. I first told her that I rob banks. After a minute of astonishment on the lady's face, I told her that I was just joking and was a tourist, doing monkey business. She was puzzled by that, and I explained that I was writing about my travels and taking lots of pictures. She asked for my business card as she wanted more information on my books. I told her that I would like to return to New Zealand to visit Wellington, some north island tourist places, Doubtful Sound, and Glowworm Caves on the South Island and take the Seasider train to Oamaru. At this time, excursions to the Moeraki Boulders and Oamaru were not available.

After the train ride, I had a long walk down George Street to the university and back. I went into a couple of shops. One shop was buying and selling secondhand clothing. I asked the storekeeper what she would give me for my jacket, shirt, and pants. She said, "Do you have some clothes to wear out of the store?" I said yes, my underwear. At that, we both had a good laugh.

Later, I caught the number 19 bus back to the motel. On the way back, I got off the bus about a mile from the motel. I took a stroll through a large park called the Oval, where cricket games are played. There was a food fest going on where small booths of hot and cold varieties of food were being sold. There must have been about 150 people, mainly students, standing around eating. After my walk back to the motel, I made an early night of it.

The next morning, Friday, February 24, I went back into the city center so I could have a walk through the University of Orgeo then back to the adjoining city center. It was registration week at the university, and there were many students walking around and hanging out on the large campus. There is a small river running through the campus with little garden areas. Some of the buildings were old, but most were newer, and some were being built. A large addition was under construction to the chemistry-nutrition building that was a concrete ten-story structure. After a walk around the campus and city center, I caught the bus to St. Kilda beach.

St. Kilda beach is a beautiful long beach where only a few people were walking their dogs along the shore. It also has a nice playground next to the beach. One guy came up over the sandy hill that separates the beach and playground with hang gliding gear as he wanted to go sky soring. He told me that there was not enough wind for him to go up.

After enjoying the beautiful area and the sound of the waves, I took the bus back to the motel so I could collect my stored bag and catch a reserved shuttle bus to the airport that is some distance from the city. The small two-gate airport is nice and even has an airline lounge, where I got some good free food and drink. There was no security check, and the airport uses the runway for taxiing. The flight to Christchurch was only an hour. After landing, I took a thirty-minute cab ride to the Hartford Hotel. It is an interesting and big hotel as it has the look of a European Chalet. My room was huge, and I wished I had a whole day there instead of a very short night of three hours' sleep as I had to catch a 6:00 a.m. flight to Norfolk Island via Brisbane. These flights were three and one hours, respectively. Before the flight to Norfolk Island, I made friends with a beautiful young Japanese lady in the boarding area. She was a computer programmer in Tokyo. I asked her why she was going to Norfolk, and she replied with the same question to me. Anyway, the strange thing was that after I had boarded the plane, I did not see her again, neither on the plane nor at the Norfolk airport.

Norfolk Island has a population of about 1,800 and is approximately five by three miles in size and has twenty miles of coastline. Norfolk has rich volcanic soil from the eroded remnants of a basaltic volcano active over two million years ago. There are two islands to the south: the farthest being Phillip Island and the closest being Nepean Island. Also, on the south side of the island is the second most southern coral reef in the world. Snorkeling is popular in the confines of a protected bay with lots of sea life. Norfolk has a subtropical climate, very rarely falling below fifty degrees in winter or rising above eighty degrees in summer. Most rain falls between the months of April and August.

Between about 1150 and 1450, Norfolk was home to the most westerly settlement by Polynesian seafarers. A village existed behind Emily Bay, but little is known of these people. The island had been uninhabited for some four centuries when Captain Cook, in his 1774 voyage aboard HMS Resolution, rediscovered it and named it in honor of his patron, the Duchess of Norfolk. On March 6, 1788, just weeks after the first fleet had arrived in Sydney Cove to establish the convict colony, an outlying settlement was formed in what is now Kingston under Lt. Gov. Philip Gidley King. Norfolk flourished for a quarter century before being abandoned again for a decade until 1825. The settlement was reopened and used for some thirty-one years as a place of secondary punishment for convicts from the colonies and Britain. Although it had a reputation for brutality, there were also bold experiments in reformation to prepare convicts for reentering society, especially under Commandant Alexander Maconochie (1840–1844). The end of convict transportation came at the same time as Queen Victoria's gift of Norfolk was made to the descendants of the Bounty mutineers on Pitcairn Island. In 1856, the whole community migrated to Norfolk, landing at Kingston on June 8. Ten years later, the Melanesian Mission was established on the island. The

Pitcairners and the missionaries were largely left to their own devices, relying on whaling and subsistence farming for a living. By 1897, when the administration of the island was returned to New South Wales, a new Norfolk-born generation had made the island their home. In 1902, the Pacific Cable Station was opened at Anson Bay, providing the island for the first time with communications that did not rely on shipping. Following the federation of the British colonies in Australia, the new federal government accepted Norfolk Island on July 1, 1914, as its first external territory. In 1920, the Melanesian Mission closed, and by 1927, the modern world was making its presence felt with the introduction of motor cars, followed by in 1932, the first visit to the island by a tourist cruise ship, the P&O Company's RMS Strathaird. *The airstrip was built at the height of the Pacific War in 1942, and by 1947, commercial air services were being provided by Qantas. During the 1950s, tourism grew, and the town of Burnt Pine flourished as new shops and hotels were built. The whaling industry closed in 1962 when whale populations collapsed. The restoration of the old convict buildings in Kingston began that same year. With increasing tourism and migration, Burnt Pine continued to grow over the next few decades.*

In flying into Norfolk, it is obvious that it is a small island. The two-gate airport was small but had two runways that crisscrossed and even a short taxi way to each runway. I took a hotel shuttle bus that dropped passengers off at four different hotels, and I was the only one left at the last stop, the Paradise Hotel. The hotel is nice but was really laid out in motel style. After check-in at 11:00 a.m., I went for a walk about the main street that took about an hour. The town had a couple of restaurants, some shops, hotels, a library, a bowling club, a post office, and a gas station. If I would have walked another twenty minutes, I would have been back at the airport.

I spent some time at the clubhouse. There was a sign in the club house that read, "There are no strangers in this club, only friends who haven't met yet." On Sunday morning, I went to the airport for a flight to Auckland. There is a small café at the airport, where I ordered a cup of coffee from a nice twelve-year-old blond-headed boy. I bought baseball caps for both of us. The boy told me he liked working for his mom, who had bought the café three months ago. He goes to junior high school and plans to leave the island for college. I told the boy that I was about his age when I started to work but at cutting lawns. On the flight to Auckland, I watched the 1983 movie "Risky Business, starring young Tom Cruise.

After landing in Auckland, I went to the nearby Comfort Hotel, where I got a few hours' sleep before my flight to Tokyo at one the next morning. I was lucky on the Air New Zealand seven-hour flight to Tokyo as I had the aisle, middle, and window seats so I could lie down and get a couple of hours sleep. I only got three or four hours sleep in Japan at the Mercure Hotel in Narita before my United Airlines flight back to Denver. It had been a wonderful trip.

Epilogue

After John finishes showering and getting dressed, he goes into the living room where Kim is still reading about one of his trips. "John, do you mind going down and getting my car since I would like to finish reading about your trip to New Zealand? I will meet you at the entrance to the building in about ten minutes, and will be sure to lock your apartment before I join you.

"No problem, Kim."

As Kim finishes reading about John's trip, she hears a loud explosion, and the building shakes. She runs to the balcony and sees that her car is blown apart and on fire in the parking lot. She screams, no, no, John was in the car. She frantically runs to the elevator. After it arrives a couple of minutes later, she takes it down to the ground floor. As the elevator is slowly descending, she is hysterically crying and thinking that the car bomb was meant for her. She cries out, "John, I am so sorry. I love you and wanted to marry you." She knows that it was probably Felex who placed the bomb in her car since he was the one trying to kill her and certainly the same one who murdered her husband in Kiev.

While Kim is in the elevator, firemen arrive at the car and quickly put out the fire. As Kim is leaving the elevator, the firemen discover the burned remains of a man in the demolished car.

Acknowledgments

I would like to thank the staff at Xlibris for their professional assistance during the production of *The Fifth Bear Hug*.

About the Author

Dr. James D. Navratil was educated as an analytical chemist at the University of Colorado and is now professor emeritus of environmental engineering and earth sciences at Clemson University. His other teaching experiences include serving as a chemical training officer in the U.S. Army Reserve, teaching general chemistry at the University of Colorado, and teaching chemical engineering and extractive metallurgy subjects at the University of New South Wales, Australia, where he also served as head of the Department of Mineral Processing and Extractive Metallurgy. In addition, he was an affiliate professor at Clemson University, the Colorado School of Mines, and the University of Idaho as well as a visiting professor at the Technical University in Prague.

Dr. Navratil's industrial experience was acquired primarily at the U.S. Department of Energy (DOE) Rocky Flats Plant and through his assignments with the International Atomic Energy Agency (IAEA), Chemical Waste Management, DOE's Energy Technology Engineering Center, the Idaho National Engineering and Environmental Laboratory, Rust Federal Services, and Hazen Research, Inc.

Dr. Navratil earned numerous honors, including a Dow Chemical Scholarship, the annual award of the Colorado Section of the American Chemical Society (ACS), Rockwell International Engineer of the Year, two IR-100 awards, and three society fellowships. He was a member of the IAEA team awarded the 2005 Nobel Peace Prize and in 2006 received the Lifetime Achievement Award for Commitment to the Waste-management, Education and Research Consortium (WERC) and to WERC's International Environmental Design Contests.

Dr. Navratil has four patents to his credit and has given more than 450 presentations, including lectures in more than one hundred countries. He has coedited or coauthored nineteen technical books (most recently with Fedor Macasek, *Separations Chemistry*, and with Jiri Hala, *Radioactivity, Ionizing Radiation, and Nuclear Energy*), published more than 250 scientific publications, and has served on the editorial boards of over a dozen journals. He was instrumental in the founding of the journals *Solvent Extraction and Ion Exchange* (serving as coeditor for many years) and *Preparative Chromatography* (serving as editor) as well as the ACS's Subdivision of Separation Science and Technology (SST) and its award in SST and DOE's Actinide Separation Conferences and its Glenn Seaborg Award in Actinide Separations. Dr. Navratil has also organized or co-organized many conferences, symposiums, and meetings for the ACS, DOE, and IAEA.

He is a diamond member of the Traveler's Century Club (www.travelerscenturyclub.org), having visited 307 countries and territories on the club list of 327. Some of these travels are described herein.

Summary

The Fifth Bear Hug is a continuation of the stories in *The Bear Hug*, *The Final Bear Hug*, *The Third Bear Hug*, and *The Fourth Bear Hug*. The story in the latter book begins with Dr. John James Czermak wanting to start a new life because he was responsible for his third wife getting murdered. He retires from Clemson University, sells his two homes in South Carolina, and moves to Colorado. John then starts working as a part-time professor at the University of Colorado and shares an office with a visiting professor from Moscow. Lara Medvedev and John start traveling together to meetings, and a loving relationship develops. They attend a conference in Sweden, followed by an expedition on a ship down the coast of Norway. From Oslo, they fly to Saint Petersburg, followed by a train ride to Moscow so John can meet Lara's parents. After their arrival in Moscow, John visits a good friend at the Academy of Sciences, where they go to the roof of a tall academy building so John can take some pictures. Then Alexei, who believes Czermak killed his brother and two nephews, shows up and tries to push John off the building, but instead, he falls to his death. Since John now thinks no one is trying to murder him, he asks Lara to marry him. She happily agrees. A few days later, they have a wedding reception at the home of Lara's parents. After the party ends and everyone has left, Lara's ex-husband arrives to kill John but accidentally kills Lara.

In *The Fifth Bear Hug*, John returns to Colorado, sells his home in Nederland, and moves to Denver. Kim Carn, a CIA agent, contacts John and asks for his help on a few missions to gather intelligence for the CIA as he had done when he was at Clemson University. Kim is also on the lookout for the person who murdered her husband, who was the CIA bureau chief at the U.S. Embassy in Kiev. She suspects he was killed because he had obtained embarrassing information concerning a White House request for the Ukraine government to find damaging information on a leading presidential candidate who was a former American ambassador to the Ukraine. The White House knows that Kim now has the information. She narrowly escapes being killed by a CIA-hired assassin who had murdered her husband. The story ends with Kim's car being blown up by the assassin with John inside the car instead of Kim.

Globe-trotters should especially enjoy reading about some of the author's travels to various places in the world.